The LENNON SISTERS

THE SECRET OF HOLIDAY ISLAND

Authorized Edition
featuring the singing stars
from the Lawrence Welk TV show

By
DORIS
SCHROEDER

Illustrated by ROBERT L. LIMBER

WHITMAN PUBLISHING COMPANY
RACINE, WISCONSIN

SOMETIMES seems like I
can still hear him of a
night, 'specially when
it's stormin' hard.
Laughin' and laughin'
like he used to!"

The old caretaker's
face took on a myste-
rious look as he con-
tinued, " . . . canyon's got a bad name from way back . . .
spirits of the massacred Injuns stuck around to take their
spite on white men."

The Lennon sisters shivered and drew close to each other
for assurance. No one had told them about the terrible "luck
of the place" until they were settled at the secluded ranch on
Holiday Island. Now they had to face it—alone!

From the very first, there was good reason to be concerned. Whose voice was it the girls heard in the storm?
Who was stealing their food? What was the reason for the
weird, indescribable screams in the night? Worst of all,
what was behind the barely averted dangers that threatened
the sisters at every step? Cut off from the outside world,
their very lives hanging in the balance, the Lennons had to
expose the *Secret of Holiday Island*.

Contents

1   *The Invitation*

The California night was starry and warm as the four Lennon sisters and their father left the big television studio and went toward their car in the parking lot.

Janet, the youngest of the singing sisters, slipped her arm through her father's and tried to match his long stride. "Gosh, Daddy, it seems funny to think we won't be coming back next week to do the show! And no more rehearsals till September, when the show starts again!"

Bill Lennon laughed. "You're not getting off that easy, young lady. You're booked for some personal appearances in August, and you'll need to learn some new songs!"

Janet gave a big sigh. "Oh, dear! I forgot. But we will be going to Uncle Max's ranch up at Ojai Valley for a few weeks first, won't we?" She sounded worried. Janet had been practicing some fancy dives just to show Uncle Max and Aunt Helen how she had improved since last summer. They had put in the ranch swimming pool just for the Lennon girls and boys.

"We always do, don't we?" Bill Lennon's eyes twinkled. He had a hunch what was on Janet's mind.

"How soon will we be going?" Kathy asked from a few feet behind. Kathy was in her middle teens, closest to Janet in age. She had a long list of friends of both sexes, and they had made a lot of plans for the summer holidays.

"Oh, you'll have time to keep a few engagements first," Bill Lennon chuckled. He knew Kathy's social inclinations. "Uncle Max is building a new bunkhouse for the boys, and it won't be ready for a week or ten days at the least."

"That's good!" Dianne, the eldest of the pretty sisters, joined in as they came up to the waiting station wagon. "That will give Mom and Peg and me a chance to shop for some summer things for all the kids."

"Including us!" Peggy laughed.

"I'll help you shop," Kathy said hastily.

"Ha!" That was Janet. "You might miss a phone call!" She grinned at Kathy, while the others laughed. Kathy was the one who had telephonitis. Sometimes it seemed to the family that each of Kathy's pals called her at least once a day. And if any of them didn't phone, Kathy did.

It was nice to have such a popular sister, but hard on any of the rest of the family who might be expecting a call!

"Hmmph!" Kathy tossed her pony tail, "I don't have any more calls than you do, Deedee, or Peg!"

"No more than five in a row!" Janet teased. But before the argument could go any further, Bill opened the station-wagon doors.

"All aboard!" He waved them in. "Let's go home and relax. Mom and Nana will think we're lost."

So they piled into the car and headed for home. And half an hour later, as they came trooping into the big, pleasant kitchen from the garage, they found Mom and their grandmother waiting for them with milk and cookies.

"How were we tonight, Mom?" Janet demanded, after bestowing a quick kiss on both mother and grandmother.

"Did you like my duet with the pianist?" Kathy asked.

"How was my solo?" Dianne wanted to know.

"Terrible!" Mrs. Lennon kept a straight face. "Nana and I tuned you out and looked at a cartoon!"

"Mom!" Janet looked horrified for a moment. But the rest of them laughed, and Janet realized that her mother had been teasing.

"Drink your milk, girls, and then you'd better turn in," Bill Lennon advised his daughters. He picked up one of Nana's tasty cookies and nibbled at it appreciatively. "It's been a long day."

"Yes, Daddy," they agreed. And in just a few minutes more, the comfortable big white house had settled into nighttime silence, and all lights were out, except one.

That was the light in Bill Lennon's study. He was reading over a stack of mail that had arrived at the house after he and the girls had left for the studio.

There were the usual fan letters, forwarded from the studio mail room in bundles, and there were invitations to the Lennon Sisters to make all sorts of personal appearances around the entire country, and for all kinds of benefits. Each letter had to be considered, and replied to after a check of the schedule of the tour that was part of their duty as featured singers with the nationally televised band.

Each of the fan letters would be answered by one of the Lennon Sisters as soon as possible. Sometimes the letters came in such numbers that the girls were swamped by the task of replying to all of them. But they tackled the task with enthusiasm, and managed nearly always to catch up before too long.

Somewhere upstairs, in the stillness of the night, baby
Anne started crying, but it didn't last long. Bill Lennon
smiled, listening to his wife's footsteps in the nursery above.
Through the long years—twenty now—that the Lennons
had been married, he had been hearing those sounds. The
Lennon children had never had to cry very long in the
night without the comfort of their mother's arms!

Bill went back to the mail. A telegram lay on top of the
penholder. He hadn't noticed it before. He slit it open and
read it with growing surprise. It was a long message, very
startling, and it was postmarked Holiday Town, Holiday
Island, California.

Am authorized by owner of large ranch here on
island to offer you and family the use of ranch rent-
free for summer, with option to buy at very low figure.
Proposition too good to ignore. Please reply collect and
I will be glad to bring full information by next plane.
Cordially,
Frank Lane, Realtor

"Wonder what the gimmick is?" Bill mused a little
grimly. "Probably another bid for publicity, using the name
of the 'Lennon Sisters'!" Bill had had to turn down a great

many seemingly honest offers which were only schemes to get free advertising for real estate ventures or other promotion schemes. "Well, this time I won't even hesitate," he growled, and started to tear the telegram across.

"Now what are you muttering about?" Mrs. Lennon's youthful face smiled at him from the doorway. "Who wants something for nothing this time?"

"Hi!" Bill grinned. "Come take a look at this wire and tell me what you think the catch is!"

She came and perched on the arm of the desk chair while she wrinkled a pretty brow over the telegram. "Why, I think it sounds wonderful! You're always saying you wish that some day we'd have a nice ranch of our own, so we could keep horses all year for the boys, and raise our own vegetables and fruit, and when the girls got married, we could build them houses of their own right—"

"Whoa, there!" Bill laughed. "We haven't even seen the place yet!"

Mrs. Lennon laughed and handed back the telegram. "Well, you wanted to know what I thought about it!"

"I suppose that means you think we should have a talk with this Frank Lane."

She nodded eagerly, smiling. "Maybe if you phoned his

office first thing in the morning, he could get here early in the afternoon."

"Why the rush?" her husband teased playfully.

"If we wait, someone else might snap up the offer! And I've always wanted to have a place on Holiday Island. Remember the day we took Dianne and Peggy over on the big steamer? Peggy was only a baby and I was afraid she'd be seasick, but she wasn't! And we took a ride in the glass-bottom boat and saw the big goldfish swimming around in the kelp beds, with the streaks of sunshine coming down through the water and making them glitter like real gold?"

Bill nodded, catching her enthusiasm. "And the seals that barked at the boat when it came close to their rocks? And that flying fish that sailed through the air and almost hit the boat before it plopped back into the water?"

"Will you phone Mr. Lane tomorrow?" Mrs. Lennon insisted. "Early?"

"Okay, you win. But let's not say anything to the girls about it till we find out if it's on the level. Promise?"

"Of course not! They'd be too disappointed if it turned out to be another publicity stunt."

But there are very few secrets in a friendly big old house

filled with healthy, happy youngsters who run in and out all day enjoying the first days of school vacation. And Janet couldn't help overhearing her mother telling a friend on the phone that they might not be going to Uncle Max's ranch at all this summer.

And it was perfectly natural for Janet to confide the startling news to Dianne and Peggy, who were busy making beds, this being their week for that chore.

"Oh, you must have misunderstood Mom," Dianne brushed it off carelessly. "I know we're going. Dad said so last night."

"Besides," Peggy said severely, "you shouldn't listen to people's phone calls."

"It was an accident, honest!" Janet assured them solemnly.

"Seems to me you had a little dishwashing to do in the kitchen," Dianne reminded her, and Janet left them hastily, knowing that when Dianne took that tone, she was in earnest and excuses weren't in order.

Peggy stopped suddenly as she was passing the window that overlooked the neat garden. "Deedee, look. Wonder who that man is with Daddy and Mom? It looks as if he's showing them a map of some kind!"

Dianne hurried to look over her shoulder through the open window.

"Wish I'd studied lip reading!" Peggy went on. "Think what fun it would be to know what people were talking about when you were too far away to hear!"

Dianne laughed. "Not me! Suppose they were talking about *me?* I might get a horrible shock!"

But the shock would have been a pleasant one, this time. Because the visitor their parents were talking to in the garden was the realtor, Frank Lane, from Holiday Island, and he was making an amazing offer to them.

"My client is so sure you will like this property, that he wants your family to occupy it as long as you wish, rent-free, this summer. And if you like it, you can buy it for practically nothing."

"I never knew there was anything but Holiday Town on the island." Mrs. Lennon's finger touched the map. "Where is the ranch located?"

"Here, on the windward side. There's a dirt road to it. Ten miles of rather bumpy going, now. I drove out to look at the place the day I received the letter from Mr. David Gardner, the owner."

"Where is he?" Bill asked.

"Mr. Gardner has lived on the East coast for the past ten years. A caretaker has been living on the ranch, but I'm afraid he's let it run down badly. The small herd of cattle have roamed wild for that time, and the place is overgrown with weeds. But the house is a fine one, beautifully furnished. I think you'll find it big enough for your family, and then some. It's been boarded up securely, except for the small room behind the kitchen where the caretaker has lived."

"Why has Gardner stayed away so long?" Bill asked thoughtfully. "What's wrong with the place?"

The agent looked grave. "I imagine you must have read about it when it happened—that must have been twelve or so years ago. The mainland newspapers carried the story on the front page. Mr. Gardner lost his wife and four-year-old child when a sudden storm overturned their power-boat, only half a mile from shore. You see, the ranch is on the windward side of the island, facing the open sea, and in winter the storms hit hard. He didn't know enough about operating the boat, so he blamed himself for the tragedy. He left for the East as soon as he could and he's never returned."

"Oh, the poor man!" Mrs. Lennon's eyes filled with

sympathetic tears. "How terrible he must have felt!"

"I'm afraid he still does," the agent agreed. "He writes that he never wants to see the place again."

"But why is he making *us* this offer, free rent all summer and a low selling price?" Bill was too good a businessman not to want to know all the "catches." "What's the angle? And why *us?*"

"You folks may think it's farfetched, but really it is quite simple," Lane told them seriously. "For over a year now, Mr. Gardner wrote me, he has been watching and listening to your girls sing on television. His wife used to sing a lot, and her voice was like theirs, sweet and true. He even thinks that one of them looks like her! And when he read about your fine big family and the fun they always have together, he thought the ranch would be just the spot for them to spend their summers. So he got in touch with my real estate office on the island, by mail, and asked me to hunt you up and make you the offer. There's only one condition Mr. Gardner would like to make. But even that could be forgotten, if you feel you don't want to be bound by it."

"What's the condition?" Bill Lennon asked quietly.

"Old Ben Taggart has been caretaker so long that Mr.

Gardner hopes you'll agree to let him stay on in that job. He's an islander, and pretty gruff, and I've heard he's pretty fast with a shotgun when kids take a notion to prowl around the place looking for mischief to get into. They say he's peppered more than one intruder with rock salt in the seat of the pants."

"Seems to me he's just carrying out his job!" Bill said thoughtfully.

"That's how I feel too," the agent agreed.

"Well, if we decide to stay there this summer," Bill promised, "we'll certainly keep Taggart on."

"That's great!" Mr. Lane rose, beaming. "Now how soon do you folks think you'd like to come and look the place over? I'd like to wire Mr. Gardner about it."

"Suppose we say the first of next week?" Bill Lennon looked to his wife, and she nodded eager agreement. "Monday."

"Splendid!" Lane beamed. So they shook hands, and the real estate agent started toward the gate. But he stopped suddenly, with an afterthought. "Oh—there's something I'd like to ask you folks."

"Go right ahead," Bill told him.

"We're having a benefit show for the new island hospital

next Saturday night, and—uh—I was hoping that if you should happen to bring the girls when you come to look at the ranch, why—uh—everyone would want to see and hear them. I mean, if they could stay over till Saturday, and just appear and sing maybe one song, we'd really have something to advertise! It would sell hundreds of extra tickets!" He waited hopefully.

"Well, I don't know," Bill hesitated. "I'll see if it can be arranged!"

"Oh, thank you!" The agent was beaming. "And meanwhile, I'll talk to Ben Taggart again, and see if he can't sort of get the place spruced up a little. I think he'll manage it, when I tell him you've agreed to keep him on. He's really a harmless old coot. Just a grouch, from living alone too long. That's his main trouble, I guess. He'll probably enjoy having a family around again."

And that was the opinion of a great many people who had seen the grizzled, scowling old caretaker making his infrequent visits to Holiday Town during the past few years.

They would have been very much surprised if they had been told the real reason why Ben Taggart made no friends among them. And Bill Lennon would have said a quick

"No, thanks" to the idea of spending even a few days on the ranch with his family!

But that was something the Lennons were to learn—the hard way!

2   *Rancho Contento*

"It sounds wonderful!" Janet exclaimed, when her parents told the girls about the offer of the ranch. "How soon will we know if we're going to take it?"

"After your mother and I look the place over on Monday," her father explained.

"I hope Uncle Max and Aunt Helen won't feel bad because we aren't coming to their place," Dianne said thoughtfully. "They'll miss us!"

"But if we have a ranch of our own, then we can invite *them* to come and stay with *us!*" Peggy offered.

"That's right," their father agreed. "But let's wait till we've seen the ranch, and not go jumping to conclusions. It may be hopeless, after a dozen years of neglect. It may be worthless to us, if it's so run-down that it'll cost a fortune to make it fit to live on. But we'll soon find out."

Mrs. Lennon looked at the eager faces around the lunch table. "You know," she told her husband, "I have so much to do here next week, shopping and all, that maybe it would be better if you took the girls to the island to look at the ranch, Bill."

"Oh, Daddy, will you?" Kathy asked excitedly.

"Well . . ." Bill Lennon smiled at his wife. "I know what's on your mother's mind: that Hospital Benefit that Mr. Lane mentioned! Isn't it?"

"It would be a nice thing for the girls to appear," she admitted, "especially when Mr. Lane took the trouble to fly over to make us the offer of the ranch."

"They may have some plans for the week," their father said. "What about it, girls?"

"Not me! I haven't a thing to do!" Dianne told him quickly. "Just shopping, and I can do that later."

"Count me in!" Peggy agreed. "I've always wanted to see Holiday Island again. I can't remember my other trip!"

"How about you, Kathy," Mrs. Lennon teased, "would you mind missing a few dozen phone calls from your pals?"

"I guess they'd call again," Kathy laughed.

"Besides," Janet grinned impishly, "half the high school spends its summer on the island, they say!"

The four girls could hardly wait to get to the airport on Monday morning. They were all seasoned air passengers and loved to fly.

They waved good-by to the rest of the family, who had come along in the station wagon to watch them take off, and then the silvery amphibian's motor roared its farewell to the mainland and took off.

"How long before we get to Holiday Island?" Janet asked the young copilot, as he came back to see that everyone was comfortable. "Do we have lunch aboard?"

Jim West smiled and his eyes twinkled as he told her, "I'm afraid you'd have to eat in a big hurry! We'll be landing in sixteen minutes."

"That soon?" Janet was disappointed. But as usual she had brought along one of her favorite candy bars, and she went to work on it without losing any time.

"You folks staying long?" Jim asked Bill Lennon, as the roar of the motors turned into a steady hum and the plane leveled off at a few thousand feet above the shining ocean.

"It all depends on what we find when we get there," Bill told him. "Maybe you know the place we're headed for. It's a ranch on the windward side, belonging to a man named Gardner."

"I've heard it talked about," the young copilot said. "But I've never seen it. Deserted, isn't it?"

"Not exactly, I hope," Bill grinned ruefully. "Just what have you heard?"

Jim West shrugged. "It's about ten miles across the island, on a road that only the wild goats ought to use. Man who owned it called it *Rancho Contento* and put up a big place. He was going to raise blooded cattle. Even imported some Brahma bulls for breeding. Then . . . well, I don't know the details, but there was a bad accident and he gave up the whole deal and left the island."

"I've heard about the accident," Bill admitted. "A storm wrecked his cruiser, killed his wife and child."

The copilot shook his head grimly. "Tricky waters on that side of the island. Even the commercial fishermen keep well out to sea to avoid the rocky coast. I guess poor Gardner didn't know his way around."

A buzzer sounded, and the copilot went up front for a word with the pilot.

"Look! The mist is clearing, and there's the high peak we can see from the mainland on a clear day," Kathy exclaimed.

"Eagle Mountain dead ahead," the pilot's voice came

over the loud-speaker, "highest point on the island. No water there, and very little on the rest of the range. Wild goats, descended from a handful left by Father Torquemada in the early seventeenth century, roam the slopes. They are very dangerous and are hunted in season. Wild boars, native to all the Channel Islands, are also plentiful. And dangerous." He sounded bored with his routine spiel.

"I've seen pictures of the boars, with tusks that long!" Janet whispered to Peggy, illustrating with her hands held at least a yard apart. "Ugh!"

"Don't worry, sis," Peggy grinned, "we'll stay clear of all the wild life. There are probably miles of barbwire around the ranch to keep them out."

"We will now turn, to make our run along the shore to Holiday Town," the pilot's voice droned on. "Fasten your seat belts, please."

The plane turned and swooped lower to fly along the lee shore of the long island. The girls peered down at the tops of the chaparral-covered hills, so close below the plane at times that they could make out an occasional wild goat fleeing into the brush.

"Indian Canyon, below," came another announcement from the pilot, "was once the site of a Chumash Indian settlement. They vanished mysteriously a century ago, supposedly slaughtered by pirates who preyed on ships that passed on their way to the settlements of the northern California coast."

Just a few minutes later, the plane was passing low over the outlying streets of the rambling vacation town. And then it turned and circled seaward, to come down in a graceful landing on the water at the end of the big pier at the center of the crescent bay.

"Looks like there's a reception committee waiting," Jim West nodded toward a knot of men on the pier, all staring expectantly at the plane as the pilot silenced the big motors.

Bill Lennon peered out and grinned. "One of them is Frank Lane, the real estate agent. But I don't know the others."

Jim West chuckled. "Only the mayor, the chief of police, the president of the Yacht Harbor Commission, and—"

But Bill had heard enough. "Never mind the rest! I can imagine. That Lane is quite a booster!"

The girls gathered their bags and wraps to disembark, and Dianne led her sisters up the gangplank, where they were all immediately engulfed in introductions to the important citizens who had gathered to welcome them.

The *Holiday Town Telegram* had a reporter and a photographer on hand, and the girls had to pose for several pictures before they were free to go with Frank Lane and their father to Mr. Lane's waiting car.

"I hope you don't mind the publicity, Mr. Lennon," Lane told him apologetically. "I just happened to mention that the Lennon Sisters might be coming to the island for a short visit, and that was all!"

"That's all right, Mr. Lane, they're used to it by now!" Bill assured him, as he helped the girls into the car.

But by the time the car had bumped slowly over the heavy planks of the pier to the wide street that outlined the curve of the bay with its banks of brilliant red geranium bushes, word had gotten around. And they made slow progress through the enthusiastic crowds of teen-agers who lined the way, calling out greetings, running to get autographs, cheering the girls individually, and getting into Mr. Lane's way as he tooled the car along cautiously.

When they were clear at last of the young enthusiasts, Mr. Lane gave a sigh of relief. But there was a lot of pleased satisfaction mixed in with it. "They'll all want tickets for the benefit, if they think you'll be staying over to sing!" he told the girls hopefully.

And Bill good-naturedly put him out of his suspense by telling him that they would appear at the benefit.

Lane was so delighted to hear it, that he was beaming from ear to ear as he drove off the wide, paved street and up a side road toward the mountains. It was a narrow road, but smooth for a short distance, as it passed the last, old houses of the original settlement, all of them shaded by huge eucalyptus trees and the lacy leaves and bright red berries of ancient pepper trees with their gnarled, massive trunks.

But these signs of civilization gave way abruptly as they passed the last of the ramshackle buildings and reached the end of the paved road.

"Indian Canyon Lane" a weather-beaten sign proclaimed. And it was very little more than a lane into which the shiny new car turned, to bump along for the next eight miles or more.

"Gardner had this road built to his ranch," Mr. Lane called out between jolts. "It needs a little fixing."

In the back seat, the girls exchanged looks. They were hot and dusty, and every time the car hit a rut, they were thrown together in a scrambled heap. It was funny at first, but it got monotonous!

"Would it be better to walk?" Janet asked a little weakly, as the car hit a particularly deep rut and she bounced almost off the rear seat.

"Only a little farther, now! We'll come to the gates around the next bend. Watch for the chimneys! There are four of them!" Mr. Lane instructed cheerfully.

And suddenly, there were the iron gates, and in a park-like clearing beyond them, reached by a winding drive-way, the big white house stood towering above the trees. Its windows were boarded, but the wide entrance door was open. A man was standing in the doorway, watching Mr. Lane's car as it turned in from the road.

"That's old Ben Taggart, the caretaker," Lane told Bill Lennon. "He's gruff and might give the impression that he's unfriendly, but don't pay any attention to that. I'm sure he'll warm up, once he has people around him again! He actually smiled when I told him you would be glad to keep him around if you folks decided to take the place for the summer."

"Nice of him!" Kathy whispered, with a grin, to Dianne. "But how did Mr. Lane see that smile, behind that walrus mustache?" And they both giggled, for Mr. Ben Taggart's drooping mustache was a prize specimen that gave him the

mild and harmless look of The White Knight of *Through the Looking Glass.*

But old Ben Taggart's thoughts were anything but mild and harmless, as he scowled at the approaching car. The coming of these strangers was more than a nuisance to the caretaker. It was a threat to some big plans that had promised to make him rich. And he had no intention of giving up those plans without a struggle.

He moved forward, a broom held in his hand as if he had been busily getting the place ready, and met the car in front of the house.

It was an effort for him to bow and smile and help the four excited girls and their father carry their bags into the big dark hallway.

"I rather expected you'd have *some* of the boards down off the windows. It's quite dark in here," Mr. Lane told Taggart in mild reproof.

"Won't take a minute to knock 'em off," Taggart said apologetically. "Maybe Mr. Lennon and you would give me a hand. I've been having a spell of trouble with my back, last few weeks. Can't do too much liftin' and haulin'." There was a whine in his voice.

Bill Lennon peeled off his coat and hung it on the back

of a chair. "Let's get started. Girls, why don't you just leave your bags here till we open up some of the rooms? Walk around outside and see how you like the place."

They didn't need a second invitation. All four of them hurried out to the porch and looked about.

"There's the ocean!" Janet stood on tiptoe and pointed over the hedge that closed in the weed-grown lawn. "And that must be the private pier Mr. Lane told Daddy about!"

"I see a sandy beach. And look at the string of big rocks on the arm of the cove. They stretch right out into the deep water like stepping stones!" Peggy commented. "Bet it's fun to dive off that big one at the end!"

"Forget the diving!" Dianne advised. "You might land headfirst on a ledge or something."

"The water's smooth in the cove," Kathy offered eagerly. "Those rocks make a natural breakwater."

"No wonder Mr. Gardner located his ranch here! And I bet the sunsets are elegant!" Janet liked sunsets.

"Let's go down to the pier right now," Peggy suggested.

"Yeah, let's!" Janet agreed. "I bet the fishing's great off the end of it!"

"You can find out tomorrow," Dianne told them. "Daddy and Mr. Lane have knocked away the boards from a couple of the upstairs windows. We'd better go in and get settled."

So they went back into the house, somewhat reluctantly, but very curious, too, about what they'd find there when the sunlight came in for the first time in over ten years!

When they had disappeared from the porch, a slim sun-browned boy in faded denims and a torn shirt rose from where he had been crouching behind the hedge, and ran swiftly down to the beach.

He plunged into the waves and swam strongly, straight out into the sea. For several minutes, his bobbing head and stroking arms were visible in the water.

Then, suddenly, he was gone. He did not reappear.

3   *From the Past*

Their father and the real estate agent were coming down
the wide front stairway as the girls entered after looking
over the surroundings of the big ranch house. Both men had
their shirt sleeves rolled up, and looked as if they really had
been working.

Upstairs, from time to time, they could hear old Ben
Taggart hammering. But he was apparently taking it quite
easy, now that his "assistants" had quit.

"May we go up now and pick out our rooms?" Janet
wanted to know at once.

"Good idea!" Bill Lennon agreed. "And after you've
decided which rooms you want to use, there's a big closet
in the back of the hall that's stocked with brooms and dust
mops and a vacuum cleaner. You'll need them to get rid
of the dust and sand that have sifted in for ten years."

"I can imagine!" Dianne made a funny little face as she glanced about the handsomely paneled entrance hall. It was plain to be seen that even though no human beings had inhabited the house for the past ten years, quite a few busy spiders had made it their home!

"I know you'll be very comfortable here," Frank Lane assured them happily. "I've had the electricity turned on, and by now the telephone should be connected. I notified the local office."

He had no sooner finished speaking than a bell began ringing somewhere in the rear. Since most of the doors on that floor were closed, no one was quite sure just where the phone was located, so Janet ran to one door, and Peggy to another. But it was Kathy who chose the right door, the one that led into the kitchen.

"It's in here!" she called to them as she opened the door, and then disappeared into the kitchen.

"Probably my office," Mr. Lane told them, and started down the hall. "I gave them this number in case anyone wanted me." And a moment later, he also disappeared into the kitchen.

"Bet it's for Kathy! Anybody want to bet a chocolate bar?" Janet grinned.

"No one knows our phone number," Peggy reminded her loftily.

"Just the same—" Janet started, but she didn't have to finish. Mr. Lane was coming down the hall, with a rather bewildered expression on his face.

"It wasn't my office," he explained. "It was for your sister. Someone must have gotten the number from the information operator!"

"I knew it! Why didn't somebody bet with me?" Janet complained, but they all laughed at her pout.

They could hear Kathy, using her sweetest telephone voice, and giggling. Janet cocked her head to one side and tried to listen.

Bill laughed and waved the three of them toward the stairs. "Up you go to the brooms and brushes, and stop being so nosy, Jan! Kathy can get along without an audience!"

Peggy and Dianne started up the stairs, eager to see what was waiting, but Janet lingered inquisitively.

"Come along, now!" Dianne caught her small sister by the hand and drew her up the stairs. "You'll grow long ears like a rabbit's, but you won't find out a thing by listening to Kathy's conversations. You ought to know that all she ever says when we're in hearing distance is 'Uh-huh' and 'Really?'!"

"If it's who I think it is," Janet predicted darkly, "he'll gab with her for half an hour, and she'll get out of doing her share of the sweeping and dusting!"

"Not when it costs him twenty cents every three minutes!" Peggy giggled. "It's long distance here, and her pals aren't that rich!"

"Yeah, I forgot that!" Janet felt better, and went on upstairs with her two sisters quite cheerfully after all.

The upstairs hall was wide and deeply carpeted. Janet counted aloud, as she pointed to the doors that led off the hallway on either side. "Three, four, five—goodness, there are a lot of rooms to choose from! Where do we start?"

Old Ben Taggart, hammer in hand, opened the door of the room farthest toward the front of the house and came out. "Your pa's taking this room," he informed them. "It's Mister Gardner's. He figured you girls should take the rooms on the seaward side, for the view. Cooler, too, in case you decide to stay."

"Let's see what Daddy's room looks like, before we choose!" Janet hurried to investigate.

Taggart looked after her sourly. "Careful not to break

anything, miss. Mr. Gardner's got some expensive doodads in there!"

"Don't worry, Mr. Taggart," Dianne assured him quietly, "Janet will be careful."

He shook his head, grumbling into his long mustache, as Janet disappeared into the front bedroom.

A moment later there was a crash. They heard Janet's "Ouch!" of pain.

Dianne reached the doorway first, but Peggy was close on her heels. Taggart looked after them and made a sound that was strangely like a chuckle of satisfaction before he turned and went swiftly into one of the seaward rooms to resume his hammering. His attitude seemed to say that whatever had happened, it was up to them to worry about it.

Janet was unhurt. She had merely tripped on a rolled-up rug that had been left directly in front of the doorway. The room was in semidarkness, its heavy draperies drawn across the windows. Janet had failed to see the obstacle, stumbled over it, and knocked over a stand that held a globe of the world. Janet and the stand had landed on the hardwood floor with some force.

"Are you all right?" Peggy groped her way to her sister.

"I guess so," Janet admitted, but when Dianne had pulled aside the draperies and let in the bright sunlight, Janet looked at her knees hopefully. A nice big scraped spot might get her out of considerable house cleaning! But no such luck. One very small pink spot was all she could find. "I'm okay."

Dianne picked up the globe and put it back on the righted stand. It seemed undamaged except for a small dent in the middle of the Gobi Desert of Mongolia.

She looked around the room, wrinkling her cute nose in disgust. "I can see why he kept the curtains closed! Look at the dust in here! He thought Daddy wouldn't notice it, being a man!"

"But leaving things around for people to fall over! We're lucky Jan didn't break her leg!" Peggy said, turning and running a finger across the top of a handsome big desk near the window. It came away gray with dust. "Look at this! I guess we'd better start our house cleaning right in here."

In spite of the dust, it was a pleasant room, looking out across the sloping lawn toward the private pier and the glistening, constantly moving sea. They lingered, watching the waves break on the clean sandy beach in slow rhythm. Far out at sea, they could see a fishing boat.

A big leather chair, turned to face the sea, stood near a small table that held a telescope resting beside a rack of expensive pipes. It was as if the owner had just gone away for a little while. Only the dust betrayed how long it had been since anyone had sat there to watch the passing ships.

In a few minutes, Janet tired of looking at scenery. "Guess I'll go find myself a room," she announced, and hurried out to start her search.

But when she had made a hasty examination of all the rooms that the caretaker had opened up, she came back to Dianne and Peggy, who were still looking at the view.

"I can't make up my mind," she pouted. "They're all nice and big, but nothing real *special.*"

"Quit stalling! I know what you're up to!" Peggy scolded her playfully. "You're scared to sleep all by your-self! Well, I'm going to have a room to myself, for once. So don't think you can move in on me—after I get it cleaned!"

Janet treated the accusation with scornful dignity. "I'm not scared at all. You're the one that gets scared, every time you hear a teeny-weeny little noise."

"I think we'd better double up anyhow," Dianne said with a smile. "You and Janet, Peg, and Kathy and I. Then, if any of us hears any strange noises, we'll have somebody to wake up!" She laughed.

"Okay, I guess I'm stuck!" Peggy agreed.

"*I* never hear noises," Janet insisted. "I don't see why I can't have a room to myself!"

Her sisters exchanged exasperated glances, and then Dianne gave in, with a sigh. "All right. But pick one fast, and then hop into your slacks and get busy on the dusting, or I'll change my mind."

"I'll go see what's in the broom closet," Peggy offered. "Come on, Janet. Maybe we can dig up some aprons to slip on over our dresses and we won't need to change."

Dianne called after Peggy, "Find one for me, too. And I'll start in here." She went back to looking out the window.

But Janet was wandering around the spacious room, examining the many masculine furnishings. The glass enclosed collection of old rifles on the wall held her attention for some time.

Dianne, watching the sparkle of sunlight on the rolling water, frowned suddenly and squinted her eyes. She was almost sure that she had just seen someone swimming, a hundred yards out beyond the end of the pier. "Jan, come here and see this in the water," she called.

Janet bounced over. "What is it? A seal?"

"I don't know. Look, just over the point of rocks. Do you see someone or something swimming?"

Janet screwed up her face and shaded her eyes, but she couldn't see anything. "Too much sun. It dazzles my eyes. But it must have been a seal, Deedee. Who'd be swimming away out there?"

"I guess you're right, Jan," Dianne admitted, but she wasn't quite convinced. "I could almost swear I saw an arm come up a couple of times in a crawl stroke."

"Hey! A telescope!" Janet darted over and picked it up. But neither of them knew exactly how to focus it in a hurry, so when they finally got a fix on where the swimming object had been, there was nothing there but water.

"Gee, I'd like to catch a baby seal and keep it in the bathtub!" Janet looked dreamy. "Wouldn't the kids' eyes pop when they saw it!"

"Mom's would pop worse than theirs, I'm sure!" Dianne laughed. She gestured toward the door. "Scoot, now! See what Peg has dug up."

Janet gave up her dream with a sigh, and started toward the hall door, dragging her heels. But halfway across the room, she noticed something for the first time. There was a door half-hidden from the rest of the room by a tall Chinese screen. "Hey, Deedee! There's another door. Where do you suppose it goes?"

"Probably a closet or something," Dianne answered carelessly. "Run along now."

But Janet had to investigate. She slipped behind the screen and softly turned the doorknob. The door opened very easily and she stared into darkness. There was another room there, almost as large as the one she was in. And in the light from behind her, she began to see things in the room. It was a nursery. The walls glowed with nursery rhyme figures done in luminous paint, and the furniture was half-size.

"What did you find?" Dianne asked, coming up behind her to look into the shadowy room. As she spoke, she reached in and felt for a light switch beside the door. It was there, and a moment later the room was flooded with light from hidden wall fixtures, a light that fell softly on the group of expensive stuffed animal toys gathered on a shelf above a long table that held a miniature railroad set, complete with buildings and little people.

Janet had nothing to say, for once, but her eyes took in every detail. And when Dianne said softly, "The boy's

room," Janet only nodded sadly.

"He must have left in a hurry that last day," Dianne said soberly, pointing to a cardboard fort and a regiment of toy soldiers who were only partly set up to battle an advancing horde of brightly painted Indians. "Poor little fellow!"

Across the room, another door stood partly open. Beyond, they caught a glimpse of sunlight filtering through the sheer silk of a window drapery.

"Let's look in there!" Janet clutched Dianne's hand and drew her across the room, carefully skirting the pathetic little fort. They went in almost on tiptoe.

The caretaker had left these windows boarded, too, but there was a board missing on one of them, and it was the sunlight streaming through that opening that had drawn their attention. Now, by that same light, they could see that it was a charming and delicately feminine room.

It was done in pastel colors, pale blue and violet, and the huge canopied bed and the satin-upholstered chairs were white, with great embroidered sprays of blue violets. It looked as if it had been plucked right off the pages of the most expensive home-furnishing magazine, to please a princess.

In spite of the film of dust that toned down the fragile

colors even more, it was still a dream room. And to carry out the fairy tale illusion, both girls were suddenly aware of a faint but distinct scent of violets. It came to them on the soft gusts of sea air that billowed the dainty silk curtains as it swept in from Mr. Gardner's open windows.

"Violets!" Janet spoke in a whisper, her eyes wide. "Yummm! Say, this is a swell room! Can I take it?"

Dianne shook her head. "We're not going to disturb it. Mr. Gardner evidently left it just the way it was on the day of the accident. And I think he'd like to find it that way when he sees it again. The nursery too."

"Suppose Daddy decides to buy the ranch?"

"I'm sure if he does, Mr. Gardner will come out here long enough to pack up the things in these two rooms personally. I know *I* would, wouldn't you? They're so private. They probably mean lots more to him than anything else in the place."

"I suppose you're right," Janet sighed. "Okay, I'll find another room. But I sure do love this one!" She sniffed the violet-perfumed air and clasped her hands. "Mmmm!"

Her big sister repressed an amused smile. "We'll find you one with an ocean breeze. I'm sure it'll fit your personality a lot better!" she said cheerfully.

They started toward the hall door, but stopped as they heard a key turning in the lock. Ben Taggart stepped in and looked startled to see them.

"You figurin' to use the Missis' room?" he asked with a frown.

"No, we're going to keep it locked up just as it is. And the nursery too. I think Mr. Gardner would rather we didn't use them just yet."

Ben Taggart nodded slowly, and his frown disappeared.

Dianne pointed to the window through which the sunlight was streaming. "And if you don't mind, I think it would be a good idea to fix another board on that window, before the sun fades this pretty blue carpet."

"That's what I came in to check on, Miss Lennon. I'll bring a new board and my tools right off." But he made no move to go. Instead, he looked slowly around the room and nodded mysteriously. "I'm glad you're not fixin' to move in. She might not like strangers using her stuff."

And with that, before they could get over their amazement at his words, he turned and stalked out. They stood listening to his heavy tread as he went along the hall and down the back stairs that led to the kitchen.

"What a queer thing for him to say!" Dianne frowned.

"He spoke as if she were still alive and could have feelings about it!"

"Y'know," Janet swallowed hard, and her eyes flicked around the room as if she expected to see "the Missis," "I feel kind of that way myself, in here!"

4   *A Voice in the Storm*

"It's the perfume!" Dianne smiled. "It's giving you notions!" She was trying to be very matter-of-fact with Janet, but the old caretaker's mysterious words had made her a little uneasy herself. "Come on, Jan. Let's pick out your room. We've wasted enough time in here."

But Janet had just noticed something on the far wall of the dimly lighted bedroom. It was a tall frame with a length of heavy white silk covering it like a curtain. She thought there was probably a long mirror under the drape, but she had to investigate. She crossed to it.

"Janet!" There was a sharpness to Dianne's usually soft voice. "Where are you going now?"

But Janet had already reached the opposite wall and was drawing aside the silk curtain.

Instead of a mirror, she found an oil painting. It was a

life-sized portrait of a beautiful dark-haired young woman smiling out at her. The eyes were painted so that they seemed to be looking directly at anyone who viewed the painting from any angle.

There was a small baby seated on her lap, a baby with dark eyes and curly dark hair that made Janet think of her pretty baby sister, Anne. And at the very bottom of the painting, close to the softly draped folds of the young mother's flowing robe, sat a grotesque little clown doll in a red and white patchwork costume. It wore a fringe of carrot-colored hair, and its bulbous nose was a brilliant red that contrasted with its white streaked face and matched the scarlet of its perpetually grinning wide mouth. The colors of the toy were a startling contrast to the delicate pastel of the robe.

Janet looked up at the serenely smiling young woman's delicate features. "Golly! She sure was pretty!" she whispered.

"What a darling baby!" Peggy and Kathy had come in, cleaning materials in their hands, and Kathy was smiling at the painting. "I could hug him!"

"But I could do without that horrible little clown thing!" Peggy said, grimacing.

"It was probably his favorite toy," Dianne said softly. "I think it was a sweet idea to put it in the painting!"

"I wonder if it was still around that day when . . ." Peggy hesitated, feeling suddenly unable to put it into words while the smiling eyes of the painting were meeting her own.

"Not likely, miss." It was Ben Taggart's voice, from the hall door. He came in, carrying a new board and his hammer. He pointed with the hammer toward the painting. "He was some older when he got drowned. Close to five. Could swim like a fish too. Nothin' on land or in the water could scare that young'un. I've seen him stand out there on the lawn an' laugh at the lightning when it was flashin' all around the place!"

He studied their interested expressions, and his face suddenly took on the mysterious look he had had when he told them that Mrs. Gardner might not like strangers using her room. He spoke almost in a whisper, "Sometimes seems like I can still hear him of a night, 'specially when it's stormin' hard. Laughin' an' laughin', like he used to!"

Janet gave a little exclamation, and drew closer to Dianne for reassurance, as she stared at the old man.

He pulled at his long, drooping mustache and shook his head gloomily.

"Poor little fellow!" Dianne said soberly.

"Bound to happen. The luck of the place!" Taggart frowned, and watched them out of the corner of his eye as they all looked startled.

"What do you mean?" Peggy demanded.

"This here canyon's got a bad name, from way back. Old Injun once told me it was a hard luck place!" He shook his head sadly. "I tried over an' over to tell the mister they made a mistake buildin' here. Bound to have hard luck!"

"Why?" Dianne asked crisply. She was beginning to suspect that the old fellow was trying to scare them. He thought because they were girls they scared easily! It was probably his idea of a joke.

"Pirates. Used to land right out there in the cove. Came ashore to the springs for water, and found out one time that the Injuns had silver mines back in the hills. They massacred half the tribe right on this spot! But they didn't find the mines. Injuns blew up the mine shafts, and moved off to another spot. Claimed that the spirits of the massacred Injuns stuck around the canyon to take out their spite on white men. And bad luck, for the mister, it sure turned out to be!" He went over to the window and started examining the broken board.

"Come along, kids!" Dianne herded her sisters out of the room and closed the door firmly behind them.

"Do you believe that about Indian ghosts?" Janet asked a little doubtfully.

Dianne laughed lightly. "Of course not! Can't you see he's only trying to scare us?"

"But it's true that poor Mr. Gardner had bad luck here," Peggy reminded the others seriously. "He lost his lovely family."

"Maybe some of it *was* bad luck—if you want to blame luck for anything. But it seems to me Mr. Gardner should have listened to storm warnings before he took his family out that day."

Kathy nodded solemn agreement. "Deedee's right, girls. You know what Daddy always tells *us* about thinking things out carefully before we get involved."

"Do you think we should tell him what Mr. Taggart said?" Janet asked.

"Why not? He'll get a laugh out of it," Dianne told her.

It was at the dinner table, a few hours later, that Bill Lennon heard the report of the old caretaker's warning. He couldn't quite hold back a smile as Janet asked anxiously, "Do you think he made it all up, Daddy?"

"It may be true that the Indians had trouble with pirates here on the island. They disappeared rather mysteriously, I've read. But that stuff about ghosts comes straight out of old Ben's head, and I think I know what made him invent it."

"What was that, Daddy?" Peg and Kathy demanded in one breath.

"I'd guess that it was his idea to scare you girls out of wanting to stay here this summer. He's had an easy life of it for the past ten years, from the looks of the place."

"But we wouldn't make any work for him!" Dianne said indignantly. "I should think he'd be glad to have the place cleaned up and livable."

Peggy grinned. "Mister Gloom would rather be a hermit than face all of us Lennon kids, I bet!"

"You may have something there, Peg!" her father laughed.

"I'm going to tell Mister Gloom we don't believe that stuff about spooks!" Janet declared.

"Why do that?" her father said good-naturedly. "No use hurting the old fellow's feelings. Let him have his fun! And besides, you just might learn some real history about the island along the way."

So later on, when Ben dropped by the kitchen where they were finishing the dinner dishes, they led him on to tell them more about the troublesome pirates and the vanished Indians.

And although he went into all the gory details with a lively imagination, they managed to keep their faces straight, though they nudged each other behind his back.

Later, when he had run out of anecdotes and gone off to his room behind the kitchen, they held back their giggles until they were safely up in their father's room, telling him about it.

"You should have heard him, Daddy! It wasn't only the Indian ghosts he was warning us about, but wild cattle, and boars with long tusks that roam around in the woods and chase people! And he says there are sharks and octopuses in the water!" They were all laughing and talking at once.

"Silly old character!" Janet sniffed. "He didn't scare *me!*"

But Bill Lennon had stopped smiling. "Just a minute, kids! He didn't make up all of that. You remember that the pilot talked about the wild goats and the boars, this morning, over the loud-speaker. And it might be dangerous if you were on foot when you ran into any of the cattle that have been roaming around the ranch for the last ten years. They might attack."

"I guess we'd better not wander around alone if we do any sight-seeing," Dianne agreed. "Let's be sure to have somebody with us."

"That's a very good idea, Deedee," her father nodded. "Don't forget it, girls. And stay pretty close to the ranch, anyhow, just to be sure you won't run into any danger."

"How about the sharks and octopuses?" Janet asked.

"Those, I suspect, came mostly out of old Ben's head! Mr. Lane told me the only sharks they've ever caught around these waters have been harmless ones, and the biggest octopus was only a five-pounder. And they're not half as dangerous as a sting ray, who can really give you a painful wound if you step on him in shallow water."

"We'll watch out for them too!" Kathy nodded.

But Janet snorted. "Huh! I didn't believe Mr. Taggart!"

"Not much you didn't!" Peggy laughed. "Your hair was standing on end all the time he was telling about those Indian spooks today!"

But Janet denied it heatedly, if somewhat sleepily.

"How about bed, all of you?" their father interrupted. "You've had a long day. And I want you to make up your minds tomorrow whether you want to stay or go back. Think it over, and we'll discuss it at lunch."

And in only a little while, the big house was dark and silent. Anyone passing by on the lonely, neglected road would have thought, glancing at the unlighted windows, that it was still unoccupied.

But the silent visitor who came from the sea knew better, and kept his distance. And after a little while, he went back into the dark waters and swam away through the white caps that the wind had started to whip up on the tops of the long rollers.

The room that Janet had finally chosen was on the seaward side, next to Peggy's. It was a pleasant one, with a bed at least twice as wide as her own at home, and she rolled happily from one side to the other, enjoying the luxury, before she settled down to sleep.

But Peggy, who had had some experience with her little sister's habits, had purposely chosen a room next door to Janet's, one with twin beds. And she left her door partly open, just in case Janet should wake up in the middle of the night and find herself alone in the strange house.

It was a good thing that she had. For, long before daylight, a small figure came hurrying in, trailing a blanket after it.

"Peg! I'm scared! Please wake up!"

"Janet! What is it, hon?" Peggy blinked sleepily at her.

"C-Can I stay here the rest of the night?" the voice quavered pathetically.

"Of course! Climb right into that bed, and go back to sleep. Everything's all right." Peggy sank back on her pillow and closed her eyes.

"Peg!" There was panic in Janet's voice. She tugged at her sister's arm. "I just heard it again! Now it's outside *your* window too!"

Peggy sighed and sat up in bed, rubbing her eyes. And as she did, an ominous roll of thunder shook the windows. "It's only thunder, hon. You know it can't hurt you."

As she spoke, there was a vivid flash of lightning that brought a whimper from Janet. "Go on to bed and stick your head under the covers if you think that'll help!"

"I'm not scared of the storm, it's the voice! Didn't you hear it just now?" Her voice trembled.

"Voice?" Peggy was reaching for her robe and stepping into her slippers as she got out of bed. "I didn't hear any voice. Come on, I'll tuck you in and close the windows."

"But there was a voice! First I heard it outside my window. And I heard it again, just now, right out there!" She pointed shakily toward an open window. Peggy could see, by the next flash of lightning, that her little sister was really terrified. "Somebody's out there talking! First he talks loud and then he talks like a little boy. Maybe there's two of them!"

"You're imagining the whole thing, hon. But we'll take a look, just to be sure. And then I want you to get into bed and go to sleep." She reached out to lead Janet toward the window, but the younger girl shrank back and stared in fear at the blackness outside.

"I'm—afraid—" Janet's teeth chattered.

"You won't be, as soon as you see there's no one there!" Peggy took her hand in a firm clasp and led her to the window. "Nobody could be outside of our window, because we're on the second floor and there's no balcony. Don't you remember?"

"Yes, but—"

Peggy pushed aside the curtains and they looked out just as a vivid flash made everything daylight bright.

The lawn and the hedge were in plain sight, and there

was no one there. Peggy stuck her head out of the window and leaned out as far as she could, so she could look all around when the next flash came. "Nobody out here!" she told Janet. And at that moment, the rain came down with a sudden roar, and lightning struck a tree on the hill above the road with a mighty flash which was followed instantly by a deafening thunderclap. It shook the house and rattled the windows.

Peggy ducked in and slammed down the window, her wet hair dripping down her face. "Well!" she felt her hair crossly. "There goes my hair-do! I hope you're satisfied now there's nobody around!"

"I guess so," Janet answered meekly. "I guess I was imagining things."

Peggy sighed. "I *know* you were!" And as the thunder bombardment kept on, she hurried over and began to close the other windows, while Janet ran and leaped into the twin bed, to disappear under the covers.

"I'll go close the windows in your room and be right back," Peggy called to her, and got only a smothered mumble in reply.

She took her flashlight and marched bravely out into the dark hallway.

She found the rain whipping into Janet's room through all the windows and ran to close them as quickly as possible.

But when she reached the last of them, and started to tug at it to lower it, she heard something, just as a clap of thunder died away.

It came from outside the window, and it was a voice, a rough, commanding voice. It shouted gruffly, *"Adelante! Vamos!"*

5   *An Explanation*

For a long moment Peggy stood by the window, too shocked to move, while the rain beat in on her.

She knew there was no way anyone could be outside that window, calling out commands in Spanish. Yet she had just heard a gruff voice snap out, *"Adelante! Vamos!"* She couldn't be mistaken. She had studied Spanish in high school and had many Mexican-American friends. She had heard those two words often, as the kids at football games cheered on their teams. "Go on! Let's go!" they meant, in English. But she had never expected to hear them in the middle of the night during a thunderstorm!

Suddenly she slammed down the window and ran across the room to the hall, forgetting even to turn on her flashlight. She bumped her shins, but she kept on regardless, out into the hallway and back to her room. And long after she was safely back in bed, she lay awake for a long time, listening to every sound and trying to reason away what she was sure she had heard.

"Don't be silly!" she scolded herself mentally. "You heard a tree rubbing along the roof, or something like that. You just imagined you heard words. That's all there was to it!"

But at breakfast on the sunny morning that followed the storm, she was so quiet that her father noticed it. Janet was bubbling over with the account of her remarkable nightmare, and Dianne and Kathy teased Peg about letting Janet disturb her rest. But Peggy only smiled faintly and hastily changed the subject.

"How about catching some fish for dinner?" she challenged Janet. "The end of the pier looks like a good spot."

That suited Janet perfectly. Anything to get out of housework! So ten minutes later, armed with some neatly sliced strips of raw bacon for bait, she was marching off to the pier with her fishing pole over her shoulder, and whistling merrily.

There was a small rowboat tied up alongside the pier, but she chose to do her fishing off the end of the pier instead. So she settled down there, and dropped her line.

And for the next couple of hours she sat there patiently, brown legs dangling over the water, and waited for the big one to strike. But for all her patience, the best she could catch was a sad little mackerel ten inches long, while the sizable ones swam snootily past in the crystal clear water, ignoring her dangling bait.

She could see all sorts of things on the sandy bottom where the long strands of seaweed waved in the current. A starfish moved awkwardly along, stirring up a small cloud of sandy particles. But when a fat goldfish moved lazily around her hook, its scales glinting in the sunrays that shimmered down through the water, she jerked the bait away. "You're not good to eat," she spoke down to him, "you're just a fat old show-off. Shoo, now!" And she held her hook clear of the water till he had glided on his way through the clear water.

She took a lot of teasing when she came back at lunch time with her tiny mackerel, but she merely grinned. "Wait till you see what I catch tomorrow!" she told them. "The big ones are just not used to being fed with nice fat bacon. By tomorrow the word will be around!"

When the lunch table was spread in the kitchen, the girls and their father gathered from their tasks, and Bill put the question to them. "Well, girls, how about it? Do you think you and the family would like to spend the summer here? You've had time to make up your minds."

"*I* do!" Kathy said quickly. "They'll love it! It has everything! There's even enough room for us to have our friends over to visit!"

"You would think of that!" Janet wrinkled her nose at Kathy. "Who wants a lot of high-school kids galumphing around the place?"

Dianne shushed her, but gently as usual. "I think we'd all enjoy the place, Daddy. Maybe we could rent some horses, and ride over the hills. It would be loads of fun."

" 'Specially if you ran into a herd of wild goats! Haah!" Janet grinned. "Me, I'll stick to fishing. Bet I get some whoppers this summer!"

Peggy was silent. Her father looked directly at her. "What do you say, Peg?"

She smiled vaguely. "Why, I guess it's a good idea. But we're sort of used to Uncle Max's place. Maybe the boys would rather go there. You know, the swimming pool!"

"They've got a whole ocean here!" Kathy reminded her.

"I think I'll phone your mother that we like the place

well enough to try it for a couple of weeks. I'll finish fixing up a few things around here today, and fly back in the morning to help her and Nana bring the kids over on the boat Saturday."

He started upstairs to call from the extension phone in his room, but Peggy came after him quickly and called softly, "Before you phone, Daddy, there's something I want to tell you!"

"Come along then. I *thought* you had something on your mind!"

Peggy cast a worried look toward the kitchen door, but none of the others appeared. They were having a laugh over something, and apparently hadn't noticed her quick exit. "It's about last night!" she started, as she went on upstairs after her father.

And when they were safely out of hearing distance in Bill's room, she told him about the mysterious voices that had puzzled Janet and herself during the storm the night before.

"How could you hear voices when there was no one around? Are you sure old Taggart didn't give *both* of you a nightmare, with his yarns about pirates and Indians?" Bill was smiling.

But Peggy didn't answer his smile. She looked sober as she answered, "I wish I could think so, but I know *I* was wide awake. And I'm certain I heard a man with a very gruff voice call out in Spanish. It sounded like *'Adelante! Vamos!'* and that means 'Go on! Let's go!' doesn't it?"

Bill nodded, frowning. "But there was no one out on the lawn when you both looked?"

"Not a soul, Daddy. It's really spooky, isn't it?" She looked worried. "I thought I should tell you."

"I'm glad you did. And I'm glad you didn't tell Janet you'd heard it, too."

"She thinks now that she had some sort of a nightmare," Peggy sighed, "but I can't convince *my*self!"

Bill's eyes twinkled suddenly, and he startled her with a chuckle. "Maybe you did hear voices, real, live voices! I hate to spoil the mystery, but I think I know what you may have heard."

"What, Daddy?" she asked eagerly.

"Why, yesterday when I was looking for a ladder and couldn't find one, I knocked on Taggart's door. He took quite a time answering, and when he did open the door, he seemed to be trying to keep me from seeing a short-wave radio set that he had been doing some work on. He finally admitted that he listens in all the time to the tuna fishermen away out at sea on their big boats, talking back and forth over their radios. They call in to the canneries regularly, too, to report the size of their catches and get instructions whether to stay out any longer or come in with the load. They also exchange some choice gossip, he tells me, in Spanish, Portuguese, and water-front English!" Lennon laughed.

"I guess we're lucky we didn't hear more!" Peggy giggled.

"Taggart said it got pretty lonesome, being a caretaker on an abandoned ranch, and in winter his short-wave set was all that kept him from quitting the job!"

"Well, at least it wasn't spooks of old-time pirates that we heard!" Peggy laughed. Then she grew serious, "But how was it we heard the voices, when Mr. Taggart's room is so far away, back of the kitchen?"

"He probably had the power turned high, because of the noise of the storm."

Peggy nodded her understanding. Then, "Do you think I ought to tell Janet she really did hear voices?"

Bill Lennon thought a moment. Then he shook his head. "I think it would be better if she keeps on thinking she had a nightmare. Knowing her curiosity, I'm afraid that she might pester the old fellow into letting her operate the thing. And if she accidentally did something to put it out of commission—good night!"

But Ben Taggart's powerful short-wave set was already out of commission, and it had been for the last two days, since a tube had suddenly burned out somewhere inside it.

Not a sound of any sort had come out of the set in forty-eight hours, either from the busy and gossipy tuna clippers far out at sea, or from a certain other trim ship for whose message Taggart had been waiting impatiently for the last ten days!

So Bill Lennon's guess about where the mysterious voices had come from was not the right one. Peggy and Janet *had* heard voices in the storm, but those voices had had nothing to do with the schemes of Ben Taggart.

As a matter of fact, the old caretaker would have been just as surprised and mystified as the girls, if he had heard those voices!

But her father's explanation seemed so logical and believable to Peggy, that she accepted it without question, and dismissed the thought of last night's scare from her mind with a little inward chuckle at her own expense.

They were all busy the rest of the day, getting the big ranch house ready for the weekend arrival of their mother and Nana and the younger children.

It took several consultations before all four of the girls agreed on who was to occupy which of the big, well-furnished bedrooms, but at last they had it all worked out and approved by their father. All that remained was to dust all the rooms, make up the beds, wash a few windows, and wait.

They were all glad to tumble into their beds directly after the dinner dishes were cleaned up, but they didn't mind being good and tired. They could take it easy for the next few days, swim or hike or just loaf.

And in the morning, all four were full of eager plans which they discussed at the breakfast table.

Bill Lennon found a moment to speak to Peggy alone. "Any more spooky voices last night?" he asked, smiling.

Peggy grinned back. "Not even a whisper, Daddy. We all slept right through."

So Bill prepared to go to Holiday Town to catch the morning plane for the mainland. But there was something he still had to attend to.

"Girls!" he interrupted a lively discussion between Kathy

and Dianne about what they would all wear to the hospital benefit on Saturday. "You're not even going to be there, unless you do some rehearsing!"

Janet groaned softly. "Can't we just do something we've already done?" She had planned to have a long day with her fishing rod. "How about 'Pink Roses'? We can do that in our sleep!"

"And that's just what it will sound like if you don't go over it a few times! Let's run through it now."

There was no "almost" learning a song for Bill Lennon. He was the girls' only teacher, and his methods were thorough.

The girls would break into their natural harmony, when learning a new song. Then they would sit down with their father and work out an arrangement. Bill would help with their interpretation, criticize their diction, suggest better phrasing, and so on.

Once they knew their parts, he would tape-record the song and play it back for correction. Then he would re-record and re-record until they blended perfectly. And that's the way they would sing that particular song from then on. Unless, of course, someone's mind was on fishing —or a telephone call that had been promised!

But it was only a few minutes before they had the whole thing firmly set, that morning.

"Pretty good, kids! We'll use that for your first one. There are three tapes up in my bag that you can work on, too, in case the benefit audience gives you a chance to steal an encore or two!" He was teasing them. He knew as well as they did that they would be lucky to get off with only three encores!

"We'll be on our toes by the time you and the family get here Saturday, Daddy," Dianne promised.

"And you'd better have a few dozen cookies baked and ready too. The boys are bound to be half-starved after the trip over on the boat!"

"You can count on it!" Kathy laughed. "We'll whip up a batch today as a starter."

Ben Taggart stuck a gloomy face in at the door. "You better get going, Mr. Lennon, or you're liable to miss your plane."

"I'll get my bag and be right with you," Lennon told him, and hurried upstairs.

But it wasn't till they were well on their way to town in Taggart's ancient jalopy, that the caretaker brought up the question that was on his mind.

"You folks plannin' to stay all summer?" he asked cagily, over the rattle of the old car.

"Don't know yet," Lennon told him. "We have to see how we like it the next week or two."

Taggart scowled uneasily, but dropped the subject, and instead began complaining about the slippery road which hadn't yet dried out after the rain. But he managed to keep the car on the road and they were soon on the main highway and into Holiday Town itself, in time for the plane.

Bill Lennon paused a moment before he got aboard. "Keep an eye on the girls, while I'm gone, will you? I've told them that if they go hiking, they must always take one of the others with them for safety. Remind them of it, if you see any of them starting out alone."

"You bet!" the old caretaker said heartily. "Wouldn't want the hard luck of the place to hit your folks. I'll do my best to keep it away." He tugged at the long, mournful mustache, and shook his head dolefully.

"I'll depend on you," Bill Lennon told him cheerfully. "But they're pretty level-headed kids, and I'm not much worried. The days of pirates and Indians are a long time past, and the girls have promised not to stray off the ranch and run into any wildlife!" He was smiling as he went down the ramp toward the plane.

Ben Taggart scowled after the plane as it rose into the sky. "Kinda sure of yourself, ain't you?" he muttered. "Lucky thing for you they won't be around here in about a month!"

6   *Complications*

Ben Taggart told himself that the Lennons would be gone within a couple of weeks, but he wasn't as sure of that as he would have liked to be. He felt that he had better take the problem to the one man in Holiday Town who might help him make up his mind what to do about this sudden worry.

When the plane was out of sight, Taggart turned his footsteps toward a tiny side street where the few old houses had been converted into small businesses. The street climbed sharply up a hill that made old Ben puff for breath, but he kept on doggedly until he reached a small shack that bore a home-made sign in the window which read: RADIO PARTS AND REPAIR.

Ben Taggart's knock was a signal, two soft raps followed by a quick scratching noise on the door panel. As the door opened for him he stepped quickly inside and closed it behind him.

The man who had opened it was tall and heavily built, with dark skin and a military air. His black eyes sparked angrily as he glared down at old Ben.

"Where have you been for the last two days? Why haven't you brought any messages from the north?" The questions snapped like gunfire. There was a faint Latin accent to his words, and in spite of the rough seaman's outfit that he wore, he gave an impression of importance.

Taggart looked sheepish. "I didn't get any messages. Somethin' blew out in my cussed radio. I tried to monkey with it, but like I been tellin' you all along, Mr. Lugo, I don't know anything about that kinda machinery."

"You should have come in at once and I'd have gone right out and repaired it. We may have missed an important message from our friends."

"I know," Taggart whined, "but I couldn't get away before this. Somethin's happened out at the ranch that sort of changes things a lot. Soon as I could, I came to tell you. Your friends better not try to come to the ranch for a while. A family's moved in to spend a coupla weeks, at least—maybe more."

"Moved in? Impossible! Have you been stupid enough to rent the place, just when our plans are coming to a head?" Lugo glared menacingly.

" 'Twasn't me," Taggart growled uneasily. He was afraid of the big man's anger. "The boss back East offered them free rent to see if they like it. And if they do, he's lettin' them stay on all summer."

"Don't you realize what will happen if they are there when the men come ashore to pick up the cargo? If they even get a hint of what we are doing, they'll have the police on our necks in five minutes! No! You'll have to find some way to make them decide they do not wish to occupy the ranch. And you must attend to it at once!"

"But how?" Taggart whined. "I've talked bad luck to them, but it don't seem to scare 'em! I told 'em about the wild boars an' the goats, so they'd stick close to the house and not go snoopin' around the cabin where we got the stuff stowed."

"Good! But you had better give them something besides talk. Unless you do not care to collect that two thousand dollars that has been pledged to you for your help in our cause!"

Taggart looked worried. "I'll do all I can," he promised

hastily. "Maybe you better send your people a code tele-gram, warnin' them to hold off a couple of weeks. I'm real sure I can figure some way to handle things here."

"Good! There is too much at stake to let a few un-important vacation seekers spoil our plans!"

"Only they ain't unimportant," Taggart growled. "They're famous singers, the four that's here, the Lennon Sisters from television! And on Saturday, the rest of their family's comin' over for at least two weeks, the real estate man says!" He scowled. "Unless somethin' can scare 'em off."

"I'll send the wire at once," Lugo agreed. "I hope it reaches *Señor* Duran in time for him to postpone the sailing of the *Starlight*." Lugo poured himself a cup of coffee and offered some to the old man, but Taggart refused it politely.

Lugo seated himself at the table to drink his coffee, push-ing aside a plate on which there were still remains of break-fast. Taggart asked, "Where's Bernardo's kid? Has he got some kind of a job?"

Lugo scowled. "He ran away last week!" he snapped.

Ben Taggart looked worried. "Won't he be likely to gab about what you're up to?"

Lugo shook his head. "He has no idea of it. Do you

think I would be so careless as to let him know anything? If Bernardo were in this with us, it would be another story. But my sainted cousin is above such matters as making himself a quick fortune!" He smiled wryly. "So I told him nothing of what I had in mind. And he went happily on his way to Mexico and left his beloved brat in my care."

"What made the kid run away? Few times I saw him, seemed like he wasn't the wild kind any more than Bernardo."

Lugo's eyes went to a long leather razor strop that hung from a nail on the wall. His smile was cruel. "Shall we say that there was a difference of opinion between Juanito and myself? Bernardo has coddled him. He is lazy. He prefers to swim and lie idly about, teaching nonsense to that noisy bird of his!" He scowled darkly. "He'll work when he comes back, or he won't eat!"

"Suppose he never shows up? What are you goin' to tell your cousin Bernardo when he gets home from Mexico, if the kid don't come back?"

"He will come back!" Lugo's eyes narrowed. "I have seen to that. I have told the police that the boy is a thief, that he ran off with fifty dollars from my cash box. They are looking for him, and when they find him and bring him back to me—" he paused, and his eyes flicked again to the razor strop, "we shall have a little understanding, Juanito and I. And after that there will be no more nonsense. I think I shall also wring the neck of that devilish bird of his!"

His words sent a little shiver down old Ben Taggart's spine. He remembered Bernardo Lopez's boy, Juanito, as a slight little fellow who was forever tagging at the young fisherman Bernardo's heels. Bernardo always took the youngster out on the boat with him, and was very proud of the boy's devotion to him.

Hard working, deeply religious, Bernardo Lopez was a very different sort of man from his cousin Chris Lugo, the adventurer who lived for excitement, legal or illegal. Because there was no evil streak in Bernardo, he failed to recognize it in his cousin. He had gone happily on a visit to his mother in Mexico, leaving the boy in Chris Lugo's care till his return.

All the waterfront fishermen knew that Bernardo hoped to bring home with him a bride "who will be a good mother to the little fellow." They wished him well, and felt sorry when he had gone, to see Chris Lugo drinking up the money Bernardo had left for the care of his boy. But they had said nothing to Chris Lugo about it. No one cared to make him angry. His fists were too powerful.

But more than one of Bernardo's friends gave a sigh of relief when the word went around that Juan Lopez had run away from the Lugo house, and they hoped he would stay out of sight until Bernardo returned.

Ben Taggart's thoughts were interrupted as Chris Lugo slammed down his empty cup and rose to his feet. "I've got a couple of cases of *groceries* in my fish shack on the old pier. Better pick them up and take them out with you. I'll be out later, soon as I get an answer from my wire to the north."

"Why can't you bring them out tonight, when it's dark? Supposin' one of the girls sees the boxes before I can get 'em into the cabin? What am I goin' to tell her is in 'em?" Taggart asked worriedly.

"That's up to you. And don't forget that it won't be very pleasant for that family, if they happen to run into our people when they come ashore for the cargo. Anything can happen if they get in our way."

All the way back to the ranch, a little later, Ben Taggart thought of ways that he could discourage the Lennon girls from wanting to stay on at the ranch. He was glad he had

told Chris Lugo about them, and that now Chris was sending word to his people in the North to warn them that the ranch would be occupied by strangers for a couple of weeks.

He couldn't make up his mind between a couple of scary tricks he had thought of to frighten the girls without doing them any real harm, but had pretty well decided by the time he arrived. Tonight, he would try it.

As usual, Janet was down on the end of the pier trying to entice a fat bass to nibble at the bacon on her hook. But it was a warm day, and apparently all the good-sized fish had breakfasted and lunched by the time she started fishing. Tomorrow, she decided, she would get an earlier start.

She didn't even notice the dark curly head that rose from behind a giant rock out at the end of the long spit of sand that stretched out into the sea on one side of the private cove. The dark eyes that watched the little fisher were friendly and sympathetic, especially when their sun-browned owner noticed that so far Janet hadn't pulled in a fish.

He looked at the plump fish his spear had captured, and seemed tempted to offer it to the empty-handed girl, but the sudden sound of an ancient car coughing and sneezing its way through the ranch gates stopped him. Instead, he plunged into the water with his spear and his fish, and swam swiftly away.

Kathy and Peggy were in the kitchen baking up a batch of cookies to put away for the youngsters who would arrive on Saturday morning.

Of course, the cookies might not be as light and tasty as Nana's, but they would do as a stopgap till Nana got around to making their favorites. "And won't both Nana and Mommy love this big gorgeous stove?" Kathy sighed, patting the glistening stainless steel monster. "It can do everything but knit a sweater!"

"Hi, here comes Mister Gloom in his ancient jalopy," Peggy looked out the open kitchen window. "And look at the long face on him! Bet somebody shortchanged him!"

Kathy looked over her shoulder and had a hard time suppressing a giggle. He *did* look glum.

Ben Taggart got out of his parked car and came toward the kitchen door.

They hurried to busy themselves, as he opened the door and peered in, tugging at his mustache apologetically. "Sorry to bother you young ladies, but there's somethin' I got to get from the drawer there." He nodded toward the corner cupboard.

"Why, come right in, Mr. Taggart, and help yourself. Wouldn't you like a cooky? They're still warm!" Peggy smiled her friendliest, as she held out the cooky jar to him.

"No, thank you, ma'am." Taggart walked quickly to the drawer and rummaged in it noisily.

"Did Daddy get off all right on the plane?" Kathy asked.

"Yes, miss," Taggart nodded. "Right on time. Hope nothin' happens to any of you whilst he's gone. He said to remind you not to wander out alone, and to stick mighty close to the house all the time." He stole a sly glance at their faces as he finished, but both girls continued to smile very calmly, apparently unimpressed. He frowned to himself. They could smile now, but if they were here when the *Starlight* dropped anchor, they would stop smiling!

He was angry with them as he found what he was looking for, a key ring with several assorted keys attached. He detached one key and dropped the rest of them back into the drawer. He slammed the drawer shut and turned to go, still frowning.

Both girls were watching him curiously. "Key to the storage cabin," he explained gruffly. "Picked up some supplies in town. Not room enough for them here." And before either of them could question him, he shuffled out and let the door close after him. They looked after him in surprise.

"Well! At least he might tell us what supplies Daddy ordered!" Peggy said with a sniff.

Kathy laughed. "He's used to running things without anybody around to question him! He'll have to toe the mark fast enough when Nana and Mommy come. Let him breathe the free air a few days more!" Kathy knew that her mother and grandmother would take inventory the moment they arrived.

"Okay, you win!" Peggy threw up her hands, laughing. "Let him boss us till they get here!"

"Let who do what?" Janet poked a freckled nose in at the door.

"Never mind, nosy. And where's the fish for supper?" Peggy inquired.

Janet waved the question aside glumly, but her eyes brightened at sight of the cookies. She helped herself happily. "Mmm, boy! Good!" she nodded. Then she glanced around. "Where's Deedee?"

Kathy and Peggy looked at each other, startled. They both remembered suddenly that they hadn't seen their sister for quite a while. "Why, I don't know," Peggy admitted.

"Me, either," Kathy agreed, looking worried. "Oh, gosh! Daddy said none of us should go far from the house alone. I hope nothing's happened to her."

Janet ran out into the hallway and yelled up the stairs, "Deedee! Hey, Deedee! You up there?"

7   *Two Mysteries*

There was no answer from Dianne's room, though Janet yelled loudly again for her. And as Peggy and Kathy joined their little sister at the foot of the wide stairway, they all looked solemn and a little worried.

"Shall we all go upstairs and look?" Kathy's voice had a little quaver in it. She couldn't help thinking of the spooky things old Ben Taggart had hinted at.

"Look for what?" It was Deedee's cheerful voice. She came from the kitchen, carrying a small tin pail half-filled with big blackberries.

"Oh! It's Deedee!" Janet almost shouted in her relief.

"Bright child! She recognizes me!" Dianne laughed.

"We were looking for you," Kathy explained. "Where have you been?"

"And what's in the pail?" Peggy asked.

"Big fat blackberries for dessert!" Dianne showed them. Then she cast a look of reproach at Janet. "I'd have a lot more if a certain person hadn't found her way to the blackberry bushes first! It was dear of you to leave these few for the rest of us, Jan!"

Janet looked amazed. "Me? I haven't been near any blackberry bushes. I don't even know where they are!"

"Please don't fib, Janet," Dianne said sternly. "Your footprints were all around. You're the only one of us who's barefoot, so it must have been you."

Kathy and Peggy looked accusingly at Janet, and when she turned to them for support and saw that they didn't believe her, she burst into tears. "But it *wasn't* me, I tell you! I was fishing off the pier till I came straight here a few minutes ago!"

"Then how did your footprints get into the blackberry patch?" Dianne asked as coldly as she could in the face of Janet's tears.

"They didn't! They couldn't have!" Janet sobbed. "I wasn't anywhere near it, wherever it is!"

Dianne sighed. This had to be settled. It wasn't like Janet, at all. "Come on. We'll see if your footprints are there or not, right now!"

So the four made their way, led by Dianne, to the berry patch, a weed-grown, neglected part of what had once been a vegetable garden.

Dianne stopped suddenly and pointed dramatically to some marks in the damp ground. "There!"

The other three stared. There were footprints, all right, prints of bare feet. And there were a lot of them, all around the berry bushes, quite distinct.

Janet walked boldly up to a set of them and put her own bare feet down beside them. Then she stepped back and studied the ground. "They're not mine! Look! They're a lot bigger!"

They *were* bigger, an inch longer and an inch wider.

Dianne took one look, and then flung her arm around Janet's shoulders and gave her a squeeze. "I'm sorry, Jan. I should have known you were telling the truth. You always do. But I had an idea we were the only people on this ranch except Mr. Taggart."

"I bet it was one of the kids that met us when we got off the plane!" Peggy guessed.

"Maybe he's a tramp and hungry," Kathy suggested gently. "The poor fellow was probably half-starved."

"Well, whoever he was, I hope he's gone on his way by

now. We want some berries for the family when they get here." That was Peggy, practical as always.

"Hey, there's a panel truck turning in at the gate! Let's go see who's in it!" Janet suggested eagerly.

But by the time they had reached the rear yard of the ranch, the tall dark man who had driven the truck was just disappearing into Ben Taggart's room with the old caretaker. The door closed behind them.

"Wasn't anybody for us," Janet sighed, with disappointment in her voice.

"Too bad," Kathy teased, "I bet you had your ball point pen all ready to sign an autograph!"

Dianne and Peggy laughed, but Janet tossed her head and wrinkled her nose at them. "I'm glad he didn't ask us for one. He looked like a real live pirate to me. I'd have been scared to death if he'd said 'Boo!' "

And they all went into the kitchen to make another batch of cookies and some biscuits for dinner, without having the faintest suspicion that Janet had come very close to the truth about Chris Lugo!

In Taggart's room, the caretaker cocked a thumb over his shoulder toward the girls who were disappearing into the kitchen, laughing and talking. "That's them," he told

Lugo solemnly. "Y'oughta hear them sing!"

Lugo gave a snort. "All I want to hear them do is say 'Good-by' and get off this place. And they'd better do it pronto!" He looked grim.

"I got an idea or two, how to scare 'em a bit," Ben Taggart grinned. "Coupla good tricks."

"We need something better than tricks now. My telegram came back. Couldn't be delivered. Do you understand what that means, my friend?"

Ben Taggart looked uneasy, as he shook his head. He could tell by Lugo's expression that it meant something disastrous. "What?"

"It means they've left Port Sebastian in the *Starlight* and will be here at any moment!"

"But they were supposed to let us know before they started!" Taggart stammered.

Lugo gestured grimly toward the silent radio. "No doubt they tried. But no one was listening."

Lugo strode over to the silent radio, and sat down. His sensitive fingers turned knobs and pulled plugs, while old Ben watched with a worried expression.

Finally Lugo removed a small tube from somewhere inside the set, and held it up triumphantly. "Here is the troublemaker. One small burned-out tube. It is easily fixed. I have a replacement in the truck. And then we shall begin listening for the *Starlight* to give her position."

"How will that help?" Ben asked bleakly.

"We will know how soon to expect her here, when we find out where she is at present."

"But won't the coast guard pick up any message she sends?" Ben had a hearty respect for that branch of the government.

"Of course! But it will mean nothing to them except the report of a chartered ship bound here on most legitimate business—the photographing of an adventure picture for television!"

"Well, say, that's mighty smart coverin' up!" Ben said admiringly. Then he looked worried again. "But I wish there was some way *we* could talk to them and tell them to cruise around a few extra days before they put in here to pick up the cargo."

"We are not equipped to send out messages," Lugo reminded him brusquely. "We can only wait to hear when they will land, and then see that the way is clear for them."

"Hope they make it at night," Taggart muttered. "I figure I can throw a scare into the Lennon girls that'll keep them and the rest of the family indoors after dark."

"Good!"

After the burned-out tube had been replaced, Lugo tried for an hour or two to pick up a message from the *Starlight*. But in spite of trying several wave lengths, he could get only the routine reports of the tuna boats at sea and a few pleasure yachts in touch with their land stations.

"Better tune in every now and then the rest of the day," Lugo advised Taggart as he left for the town. "Write down anything you hear from the *Starlight,* and bring it in to town right away. It may be in code and have to be translated."

Ben Taggart scowled after Chris Lugo as the big man drove out through the ranch gates. He gave a lot of orders, Lugo did, just like he was somebody! "Do this, do that!" the old man growled. "If it wasn't for that two thousand that's comin' to me, I'd back out of the deal!" But even as he said it, he knew he was too afraid of Chris Lugo to do that, money or no money.

He busied himself in his room with a certain device that he intended to use to scare the girls tonight. It was a simple contraption, but he had known it to cause a real panic under the right conditions.

When Dianne knocked on his door and called, "Mr. Taggart, we'd like to have you eat dinner with us!" he hastily hid the thing he had been working on, and hurried to the door.

"That's right kind of you, Miss Dianne. I'll be glad to taste good home cooking."

And he had a chance a little later, while the girls were clearing the table, to give them a solemn warning. "I don't figure to scare you young ladies," he told them with a worried frown, "but my friend that visited me this afternoon, he told me to warn you folks not to go outside after dark. Seems the whole town's in an uproar about that mountain lion that got away when the circus fellows was unloadin' yesterday at the pier. They ain't found the critter yet."

"A mountain lion? We hadn't heard anything about that!" Dianne was astonished.

"Gosh! Do they think it's around here?" Janet's eyes were like blue saucers.

"Don't know where to look!" Taggart shook his head. "Half a dozen folks claim they've caught a look at it in the woods, here and there. There's no tellin' where the critter may be. There are law officers tracin' down all the rumors, but so far, they haven't spotted the lion."

"I'm glad you warned us," Peggy said gratefully. "We weren't planning to go out, but we might have."

"Just as well not to chance it." Taggart was pleased with the result of his lie. He was even quite proud of himself, as he heard them still discussing the danger after he had gone outside to enjoy a pipe of tobacco.

Dianne's voice came quite clearly to him as he paced up and down near the open kitchen window. "It's a good thing Mr. Taggart told us about that mountain lion. I was thinking of all of us going for a moonlight swim in the cove tonight! Br-r-r!"

"Hope I don't have another nightmare!" Janet said soberly. "But I bet I do!"

Ben Taggart smiled to himself. She might not have a nightmare, but he could pretty well guarantee that she wouldn't have a peaceful night!

It was well past midnight when the sound of a wailing cry woke all four of the girls in their rooms.

Dianne and Kathy sat up in their twin beds, and called to each other, "What was that?"

It came again, an unearthly screaming somewhere out in the darkness. The sound rose and fell, then died away.

The door of Dianne and Kathy's room burst open a

moment later, and Janet dashed in with Peggy close after.

"Deedee! What was that? Did you hear it?" Janet's teeth were chattering.

"Of course we did! Switch on the light and close the door!" Dianne tried to sound calm, but her voice shook as much as Janet's had, as she got out of bed.

"It must have been that mountain lion!" Peggy closed and bolted the door behind them as Janet threw the light switch. "It was horrible!"

"Well, it can't get through these windows, anyhow! I don't think they can climb this high!" Kathy offered from under the covers.

"They can too!" Janet disagreed, hopping into Dianne's deserted bed. "I've seen them in television pictures, lots of times, climbing right up into the tops of trees!"

"But why would he climb the side of the house?" Dianne asked matter-of-factly.

"He might be hungry!" That was Janet poking her head out from under the covers. "Better close the windows."

Peggy and Kathy looked at each other and at the wide-open windows, but Dianne, taking her courage in hand, marched over and slammed the windows down, one after the other. Her knees were knocking, but she got it done.

Now, as the weird screams began again, they felt safer. But not sleepy! And it was only after the strange wailing had stopped for nearly half an hour, that the three younger girls managed to settle down to a restless sleep, with all the lights on bright.

But Dianne sat up and pretended to read a book. She was thinking hard. There was something strangely familiar about the sounds they had heard. Where had she heard them before?

She was still puzzling about it when dawn streaked the dark sky and she tiptoed over to put out the lights so the girls could finish out their sleep.

8 *One Mystery Solved*

It was broad daylight when Dianne woke to find that she had fallen asleep in the chair beside the window. For a moment, she was bewildered, but the sight of her sisters still sound asleep in the twin beds brought the night's happenings back to her at once.

She rose noiselessly, and tiptoed out of the room, closing the door softly after her.

Out in the hall, she listened at the head of the stairway for sounds from the kitchen. Ben Taggart should be up and about, getting his early coffee by now. But she couldn't hear him. Maybe the weird screams had broken his rest, too, and were making him sleep late.

Then, suddenly, she wheeled and ran lightly into the big front bedroom where her father had slept. There was a telephone extension there.

She came in and closed the door softly after her. One of the window shades was up far enough to let in a little light, and she hurried across the room to the telephone.

In a couple of minutes, she had the Holiday Town police headquarters on the phone. "This is Dianne Lennon, out at Mr. Gardner's ranch," she said quietly into the receiver. "That mountain lion that the circus lost was howling around here last night. I think you'd better send some men to capture it."

The male voice at the other end of the line rose excitedly in reply.

"I don't understand," Dianne was bewildered. "We heard it give the most awful screams."

Again the male voice talked loudly, and then there was a sudden click that hurt Dianne's ear. Slowly she put the phone back in its cradle, looking dazed. "No circus and no mountain lion. And they think we're just cooking up a publicity story." She spoke out loud, trying to make sense out of it all. And then all at once she was angry, very angry, at Ben Taggart. He had lied deliberately to them and put them in a questionable light with the Holiday Town police. The sergeant who had answered the phone had been quite sarcastic about it.

"But we *did* hear those screams!" she thought unhappily. "There must have been *something* out there!"

She stared a long time at the telephone and her hand moved toward it a couple of times, only to pull back again. "I won't bother Daddy with it! We'll find out ourselves what it was all about!"

And a few minutes later, she woke her sisters and told them about the sergeant's attitude.

"Call Daddy and tell him," Janet insisted.

"Do you think we should?" Dianne asked the other girls. "I wish we could handle this ourselves. I'm sure Mr. Taggart made up that stuff about the circus and the mountain lion getting away, just to scare us. But he certainly couldn't wail like a banshee if he tried! We all know that!"

"Well, something did! And I don't want to hear it again!" Peggy looked grim. "Far as I'm concerned, I'm for starting for home this morning. I've had it, here!"

"But I haven't caught a decent-sized fish yet!" Janet protested unhappily. "I'm bound to catch one today! I just know I will!" She appealed to Dianne. "Can't we stay?"

The older girls exchanged uncertain looks. "What do you say, Deedee?" Kathy put it up squarely to the oldest. "Should she go fishing, or do we pack for home?"

"Well, as long as there isn't any mountain lion loose, I guess Jan won't be gobbled up! But I'd certainly like to know who or what made that horrible noise last night!"

"Looks to me like it was Mr. Taggart. It has to be!" Peggy decided. "And I wish we could find out somehow just how he did it, the old fibber!"

"Bet he'll never let on!" Kathy said with a grin. "He's probably laughing behind that droopy old mustache right now, thinking how scared we must be!"

"Why do we give him the satisfaction? Let's all pretend we didn't hear a thing!" Dianne suggested.

And a little later, as they were eating breakfast in the big sunny kitchen, they did just that.

As soon as he had heard them stirring about in there, old Ben had come in pretending to be alarmed over the sounds of the lion's howling during the night. "Hope you girls weren't too scared," he told them, with a straight face. "There wasn't any real danger so long as you stayed in the house."

"Why, did *you* hear noises last night, Mr. Taggart?" Dianne asked him with wide-eyed innocence. "Are you sure you didn't dream it?"

"You mean to say you girls didn't hear those awful

screams?" Ben Taggart stared at their blank faces in disbelief.

"Screams?" Kathy looked at Peggy. "Maybe we were all too tired to wake up."

Janet choked back a giggle and had to stuff a piece of toast in her mouth and pretend that she had choked.

"And you think it was that mountain lion that escaped from the circus?" Dianne asked Taggart, with a slight pucker of her forehead to show she was worried.

"Couldn't a been anything else, Miss Lennon. I'm headed for town first thing this morning to notify the police!" he assured her loudly. And a few minutes later, they were amused to see his old jalopy chug past the window on its way somewhere, but certainly not to police headquarters!

When the sound of its ancient motor had died away, they exploded in peals of laughter.

Dianne sobered first. "He really wants us to go, doesn't he? I wonder what trick he'll try next?"

"Well, he isn't going to scare us off, no matter what it is!" Peggy said firmly.

"I'm still wondering how he made that awful noise!" Kathy said seriously. *"If* he did!"

"Maybe the Barefoot Blackberry Eater did it!" Janet

grinned. "Maybe he didn't want us to take any more of the berries!"

They all laughed, and then Dianne held out the empty tin pail. "That reminds me, how about finding a few for a pie for dinner? I'll start the crust."

"Come on, Peg, let's face the thorns together!" Kathy urged, and the two of them went off cheerfully to gather blackberries.

But they found more than blackberries in the patch. Peggy saw the sun reflecting from something shiny on the ground, and was surprised to recognize the tomato can that they had opened for dinner last night. "Now, how did that get there?" she asked.

Kathy picked it up, and found that someone had bored a hole in the bottom of the can and a string was dangling from it, held by a knot, and heavily coated with some sort of yellowish stuff that was sticky to the touch. Without realizing what she was doing, Kathy tugged at the coated string and her fingers slid along it. She almost dropped the tin can as she heard the moaning sound that came from the empty can.

"What was that?" Peggy asked, shivering.

"This thing!" Kathy pulled at the string again, and this

time the low moaning sound rose into an unearthly screech, a quavering high-pitched note.

"That's what we heard last night!" Peggy exclaimed. She reached for the tin can and experimented with it, getting all varieties of screams and moans. "Hey, listen to this!"

They heard Dianne calling frantically, and then saw her come running toward them, carrying a kitchen knife. "What is it? I'm coming! Don't be scared!" she was shouting as she ran, and Janet was close on her heels.

But when she came in sight of the tin can in Peggy's hands, and saw what it was, she stopped running, and came more slowly. "So that's how he did it!" She took the tin can from Peggy and looked grimly at it. "No wonder I thought last night that I'd heard a noise like that before! One of the kids brought one of these things to Danny's birthday party. I remember Mom had to take it away from the little monster because he was scaring all the other kids with it!"

She started to fling it away, angrily, but Peggy stopped her. "Let's keep it where Mister Gloom will be sure to notice it, but let's not say a word. I want to watch his face when he sees it. He'll know we're onto his trick, but he won't dare mention it!"

So they picked all the berries they could find, and took them and the old tomato can back to the house. They set the can on a shelf in the kitchen where Taggart couldn't miss seeing it.

But they had another surprise when they looked around the kitchen. Someone had been there while they were gone, and had helped himself to the contents of the cooky jar, at least one can of beans, and half a loaf of bread.

The girls checked quickly upstairs, but found nothing of theirs missing. Evidently the intruder had confined his visit to the kitchen.

"We ought to phone the police!" Peggy wanted to do it at once.

"No, don't!" Dianne told her quickly. "They'd be sure to think we were looking for publicity, after the way they took my phone call this morning!"

"But we can't have a thief around!" Kathy protested. "He may be a desperate character!"

"Hey, look!" Janet pointed to something on the center table. "Whose are these?"

Peggy glanced at the four pennies and a large copper coin. "Not mine."

The others looked and shook their heads. "Never saw

them before," Kathy said. "They weren't here when we went to pick the berries."

Dianne examined the larger coin. "It's a Mexican penny, a centavo. That's funny! Our visitor must have left it to pay for the food!"

"Well, at least that proves he isn't a thief! The poor fellow is probably half-starved," Peggy said sympathetically.

"Maybe I better catch *two* fish," Janet was getting her fish pole out and looking for some bacon to cut up for bait. "Then if we see him we can invite him to dinner."

"I bet you won't even catch *one* that's big enough for more than two bites!" Peggy teased.

"Betcha I will!" Janet told her defiantly, "Betcha I get one so big you have to come an' help me carry it!" And she ran out and down the sloping lawn past the hedge and out onto the pier.

Dianne looked out the window toward the sky. It was filled with scurrying clouds, and some of them were ominously gray. "It looks stormy," she told her sisters, "I hope it isn't raining on Saturday when the rest of the family get here. I want them to love the place, so Daddy and Mom will decide to stay all summer."

"And won't that make our friend Mr. Taggart happy!"

Kathy laughed. "Serves him right, the tricky old character, trying to scare us off!"

"Oh, he'll give it up, after he finds it doesn't work!" Dianne said confidently. "Once he discovers what lovable characters we all are, he'll be sorry he tried to get us to leave!"

They all laughed at that. But it wouldn't have seemed so funny to them, if they had been listening to what Taggart had to say to Chris Lugo, at Holiday Town, just then.

"I tuned in the *Starlight* this mornin', just before daylight. They were makin' out like they were reportin' to some movie studio on the mainland." He frowned. "It sounded like Luis Duran's voice—"

"Yes, yes, go on! Did he say when they would arrive?"

"He said they would make some scenes on Friday at the location," the old man referred to a scribbled note that he had made of the conversation. Then he looked worried. "Does that mean they will arrive tomorrow?"

Chris Lugo nodded grimly. "It means nothing else, since tomorrow is Friday!"

"But what about those Lennon girls?" Taggart asked, "How am I going to keep them from seeing what Duran's men are up to?"

The big man shrugged, and his eyes were cold as steel. "It will be too bad for them if they see too much. And I'm afraid if things do not go smoothly tomorrow, *Señor* Duran will not be willing to pay the money he has promised you —and me!"

"I tried last night to scare them off, but it didn't work. I don't know what to do next. But I got to have that money! Duran can't blame me if there's trouble!"

"There had better not be trouble. The future of *Señor* Duran and his country rests on the success of this expedition." Lugo spoke harshly, and there was menace in his voice as he added, "Nothing must interfere."

9 *Janet's Peril*

All the way back to the ranch, Ben Taggart tried hard to think of an argument he could use to persuade the Lennon sisters to vacate the ranch at once. They hadn't been impressed by his talk about hard luck, ghosts, or even wild animals. He felt sure that they had heard the unearthly screams he had conjured out of the tin can with the rosined string, but for some reason they had decided to pretend they hadn't. What could he do now, at the last minute, to shock them into leaving the ranch before Luis Duran and his men arrived to pick up the vital cargo that was stored on that ranch?

He was still puzzling over it, when he turned the old car in at the ranch gates and drove up toward the house.

It was only by chance that he happened to notice Janet, a small lone figure sitting on the end of the pier, fishing patiently. In the west, the black clouds were boiling up, and he knew that a storm was threatening.

Suddenly, the idea came to him. So far, he had only threatened hard luck and pretended danger. Maybe the Lennons would only be convinced by the real thing. A near-tragedy, a close call for one of them, might do it! And the most likely object was little Janet.

He stopped the old jalopy near the land end of the pier, and when Janet turned her head to see who had driven up, he waved in friendly fashion to her and got out. As an excuse for stopping at the pier, he took a hammer and some nails from the car, and went out to talk to her.

"Any bites yet?" he greeted Janet as he came up and took a quick look at her empty creel lying beside her.

"Just a nibble, but he was only a baby, so I didn't let him get a good bite," she explained gravely. "I'm going to get a big fellow today."

"Don't think you'll do it, sittin' there, Miss Janet! But if you'd like, I'll show you the spot where I got a five-pounder last week. Pulled him in, just about this time of day, when the tide had just turned."

"Please show me!" Janet asked eagerly. "I've just got to bring one in today, a big one!"

"Well, it's tricky underfoot, gettin' out there," the old man said doubtfully, "but if you don't mind wadin' ankle deep on your way, you're bound to snag a big bass."

Janet was on her feet now, ready to go. "Show me, please! I don't mind getting my feet wet!"

"Well," he looked out toward the string of rocks that lined one side of the cove, "you see that big rock out there? Well, the current swings in right there, and there's a whirlpool that catches some mighty big sea bass on their way past. If you drop in a line just right, they'll grab it."

Janet lost no time leaving the pier and starting out toward the rocks, fishing pole over her shoulder. The water was only a couple of inches deep on the steppingstones that led out to the tall end rock, and Janet went carefully so she wouldn't slip on their mossy flat tops.

When she got out to the big rock, she looked back and waved to old Ben Taggart, standing on the narrow beach waving to her. For a brief moment, the thought came to her that he seemed a long way off. She had come farther out along the rocks than it had looked from shore.

But a moment later she forgot her doubts and started the climb up to the top of the rock. To her delight, she found a natural hollow near the top, like a seat. It had evidently been carved by the sea, and was smooth and comfortable. She settled herself in it and peered down expectantly into the gently lapping small waves. The water was so clear that she could see the sunlit bottom and the gently waving seaweed.

She was thrilled and excited to see a large sea bass glide by, but by the time she had baited her hook with bacon and dropped her line, he was gone. "But there are bound to be lots more, just as big," she told herself, and settled down to watch and wait.

Overhead, the storm clouds were getting thicker and darker. The waves that lapped the rocks broke constantly a little higher, till some of them were splashing handfuls of water as high as her dangling feet. But it felt good, and refreshing, so Janet didn't pay much attention to it, except to wiggle her toes happily each time the high seventh wave rolled in.

Once, a large fish that she couldn't get a good look at, because the incoming tide was raising clouds of sand, nibbled the bacon, but went merrily on its way when it had stripped the hook. "That," Janet called after it reproachfully, "was a mean trick!" and she rebaited her hook and dropped her line in again.

There was a sudden gust of wind, as a wave came against the rock and broke so high that Janet was drenched from her head to her toes. She sputtered and choked as she swallowed salt water, and struggled to her feet as the wave receded.

For the first time in half an hour, she glanced back along the string of rocks. She could still see them, but they were covered by a foot of water, and the wind was sending small waves over them.

"Better get down off here and head for shore," she told herself, while another high wave broke and drenched her to the knees as she stood holding onto the rock with one hand and her fishing pole with the other.

Then she saw her creel carried off by the receding wave. She couldn't grab for it, without letting go of either the rock or her fishing pole, so she had to let it go.

She started to climb down the rock, but the storm-raised waves were coming in too fast now and too roughly. Desperately she looked toward the shore, and caught sight of old Ben Taggart, very busy with his hammer in the small rowboat tied near the end of the pier. She yelled to him and waved, and Taggart stood up beside the small boat and waved his hat to her.

"Bring—the—rowboat!" she shouted, but the waves

drowned her shout. She saw Taggart turn his back and get busy hammering again at something in the rowboat. Then instead of starting to row to her, he climbed up to the pier. He hadn't understood that she needed help!

She called again, as the waves rolled in constantly higher, their crests whipped to a froth by the wind. Now, as the tricky seventh wave, the highest, began to recede, Janet was frightened to see that the steppingstones were completely submerged and out of sight, and the water was up to her knees, even on the high rock.

"Guess I'll have to swim for it, unless Mr. Taggart looks this way again," she thought, looking at the swirling waters with distaste. But when she glanced back toward the pier again, she saw that he was starting back to the house. There would be no help from him!

The waves were rougher, as the tide came higher and the storm broke over the cove. Rain beat down in a torrent, and the wind struck hard at her. It was all she could do to hang onto the rock with both hands. Her fishing pole floated away, but she didn't dare let go her grip on the rock to try to save it.

From halfway up the lawn, Taggart peered through the hedge toward the rocks and saw that Janet was still hanging onto the high end rock. But it was plain that she wouldn't be able to keep her grip on its slippery surface much longer. It was time for him to give the alarm. He started running toward the house, yelling, "Help!"

Dianne was just coming out onto the front terrace to call Janet in out of the rain, when she saw the old man running and heard his shouts.

She ran to meet him, as Kathy and Peggy rushed out of the house to see what was the matter.

"Miss Janet's in trouble! Look! Out there!" He pointed excitedly.

They stared, stunned, and at that very moment, a huge storm-whipped wave rolled in and swept Janet from her perch. They saw her struggle to the surface a dozen feet out in the swirling water.

All three of them started running at once toward the pier, as Dianne shouted, "Get the rowboat!"

Taggart followed, yelling, "It's no good! It's got a bad leak in the bottom!" But they ran on, desperately.

The small boat was half-filled with water. It would be of no use.

Janet was swimming strongly, but battling the strong undertow to try to get back to shore. She had seen them on the pier, they knew, because she raised one arm and held it straight up, a signal of distress that they had agreed on several years ago when they were all learning to swim.

"She's afraid she can't make it!" Peggy exclaimed. "We've got to get to her!" She started to kick off her shoes, but Dianne stopped her.

"I'm the best swimmer," Dianne said hastily, "so you two stand by here to help. I can get her." She stepped out of her shoes and made a graceful dive from the end of the pier. A moment later she was swimming toward the spot where Janet was struggling.

Janet was lifted to the top of a swelling wave, and saw her sister swimming in her direction. She tried to wave, but as she did, another surge of water struck her from behind. It tumbled her over into the deep water, tossed her around, bumped her on the sandy sea bottom, and carried her seaward, caught in the undertow.

Somehow, she managed to fight her way to the surface for a saving breath, but as she looked toward the shore hoping to see Dianne swimming toward her, she saw to her horror that the pier was no longer in sight. The shore that lay before her eyes was a strange, rocky one.

The current had carried her out and around the arm of

the land! She was alone, far from the rocky shore. She almost gave up hope at that moment, but not quite. There was a lot of fight left in her, and she battled the breakers desperately, though she knew she was getting weaker all the time.

Dianne, swimming to the point where she had last seen her little sister, lifted herself out of the water to look around. But Janet was no longer to be seen! The surface of the sea where she had been was unbroken except for the long, high swelling waves. "Janet!" The cry broke from Dianne as she realized with horror that Janet was gone.

Then the high waves caught Dianne and swept her, almost unresisting in her grief, toward the end of the pier.

Peggy and Kathy had lost sight of Janet as the undertow sucked her down, and when she didn't appear again, they were sure she had drowned.

But there was no time for tears now. They could see that Dianne, too, was in trouble. She was being tossed about by the rough waves and would be swept past the pier in a moment.

They didn't hesitate. "Let's get her!" Peggy snapped, and they dived together and struck out bravely toward her.

Ben Taggart crouched on the pier to watch. He was

frightened and sorry. He told himself, "I never meant to drown the poor kid! I only figured to scare 'em!" But it didn't make him feel any better. He knew he had gone too far to earn that two thousand dollars!

He stared miserably across the turbulent water at the two bobbing heads of the swimmers. If he hadn't knocked loose a plank in the rowboat, he could probably help them save their sister, and there would only be one drowning on his conscience.

Then he saw that the girls had reached Dianne and were bringing her in, and he breathed freely again.

But the little one was gone. Now they would be glad to pack up and leave the hard luck ranch, he thought. There would be no interference when Luis Duran and his men came to pick up their cargo.

But Janet hadn't given up yet. She was still fighting, around in the next cove, though she was getting weaker now.

It seemed, suddenly, as if she couldn't lift her arms out of the water another time. She was so tired of struggling that it would be a blessed relief just to let go and sink down, down . . . .

"I will help you! Lie back and do not struggle!" The

voice was in her ear, and at the same time, Janet felt a strong arm take hold of her. "Be calm! Lie back!" the voice commanded. She obeyed, rolling over on her back so that the mysterious rescuer could adjust his arm under her chin and tow her along with her face out of the water. "It is only a little way and you will be safe!" the voice told her confidently.

She was only half-conscious, full of salt water, and too tired to move her feet to help him float her along, but her keen young mind was still alert. "Why, it's only a boy," she thought drowsily, "and he has a Spanish accent!"

Then she drifted into unconsciousness.

10   *Juan the Runaway*

"How do you feel now, miss?" It was a stranger's voice, with a soft Latin accent, yet it wasn't quite strange to Janet. She opened her eyes slowly and saw a slim young fellow in a faded blue denim jacket and pants, squatting beside a small fire over which he was heating something in a pan.

"I'm c-cold," she said, with a shiver, "and my mouth is awful salty."

"This warm milk will take care of both," the young man assured her with a pleasant smile.

She leaned back, studying him, and trying to remember what had happened out there in the water. It was all coming back gradually. She sat up suddenly, "Hey! You pulled me out of the water, didn't you?"

He gave a little shrug of his shoulders, and laughed. "I just happened to be swimming out there when you sort of floated past me. So I brought you ashore."

"Gosh, thanks!" Janet managed a grin. "I was getting pretty tired, I remember." She shivered again.

He poured warm milk into a tin cup and brought it to her. "Drink this and you will feel better."

She gulped the milk gratefully, clutching the cup with both hands at first, to keep from spilling it. And in a couple of seconds she felt warmer and stopped shivering. "That was good."

"More?" he smiled, but she shook her head. She looked around, puzzled, and saw that she was in a cave of some sort. The floor was sandy, and outside the mouth of the cave, she could glimpse the sea.

"Is this a sea cave?" she asked curiously.

The boy nodded gravely. "I live here. We are higher than the tide."

She saw a shelf with a few school books on it and a coal-oil lantern. And there were some cans of food stacked up in a far corner, and a blanket spread neatly on a pile of grass, evidently the young man's bed. "It looks comfortable," she told him. She was thinking that he probably didn't live here at all, but just came and camped out during summer vacation weekends. He was Kathy's age or perhaps just a little bit older, she decided.

"My name's Janet Lennon," she said, with her shy smile. "What's yours?"

He hesitated noticeably before he answered. "Juan."

"Just Juan?" Janet flashed a friendly grin. "Don't you have another name?"

"It is better if I do not tell you my last name." Juan looked grave. "I do not wish anyone to know that I am here, especially the old man with the mustache of a great walrus!"

"Mr. Taggart?" Janet was startled, then she laughed. "My sister Peggy says he has a mad on at the world! We call him Mister Gloom!"

"You will not tell that you have seen me? You will keep it a secret?" Juan asked urgently.

"I'll have to tell the girls that somebody saved my life, won't I?" Janet asked reasonably.

"Then say it was one John Smith. That is a good name!" he told her, with a smile. "But do not speak about my home here, or the old man will come and drag me to the police—" He stopped abruptly as he saw the startled look on Janet's face.

"Police?" she asked sharply. "Are they looking for you

for something?" This was exciting! "What did you do, Juan?"

"Nothing wrong," Juan smiled, but his eyes were troubled. "There has been a misunderstanding, but it will all be cleared up when Bernardo returns from Mexico and I can tell him what really happened."

"Who's Bernardo?" Janet asked at once.

·"My father," Juan told her proudly, "the best tuna fisherman on the whole coast." But the moment he had spoken, he looked as if he were sorry. "But you must not mention his name. Remember, you promised!"

"I won't forget." Janet could be very serious when she wanted to. "Tell me about your father."

But Juan shook his head. "It is time you were going back to your sisters. They will think you have drowned." He rose and motioned toward the rear of the cave. "Come! I will show you the way back to the ranch house!"

Janet got to her feet, feeling a little wobbly, and not nearly dry yet, in spite of the small fire. "Okay, then," she sighed, and took a step in the direction he had indicated. But as she did, she heard a voice.

"Today the fish are of good size!" the voice said in deep masculine tones. "Throw the small one overboard!"

Janet shrank back and grabbed Juan's arm. "Who's that? I thought you were alone!"

Juan laughed. "Not exactly, miss. El Capitan Pedro is with me!" And as he spoke the name, there was a flutter of dark wings, and a mynah bird flew out of the dim recesses of the cave and alighted on Juan's shoulder.

"Throw the small one overboard!" the bird repeated.

Janet stared at it, amazed, and Juan laughed again, and stroked the bird's black feathers affectionately. "He doesn't mean you, Miss Janet! He is imitating Bernardo's commands!"

"Hey, I bet I heard him outside my window the first night we were at the ranch! I heard Spanish voices talking, but there was nobody around when Peg and I looked!" She laughed gaily. "And she told me I had a nightmare! Wait till I tell her about him!"

"But you mustn't!" Juan said quickly. "Too many people know El Capitan Pedro is my friend. Do not mention it, please."

"All right," Janet couldn't help pouting a little. She would have liked to tell her big sister she had been mistaken. "He's smart, isn't he?"

"Smart!" the mynah repeated, in Janet's own voice.

Which brought a laugh from Janet and a proud smile from Juan. But Capitan Pedro had to imitate Janet's laugh and then top off his performance by standing on his head and squawking loudly.

"That is enough silliness, Capitan!" Juan told him sternly. And the bird suddenly pecked his owner's ear and then flew back into the shadows of the cave. "He's a wicked bird, sometimes," Juan admitted, rubbing his sore ear.

Whereupon, the unseen bird proceeded to call out a whole string of Spanish words whose meaning Janet didn't know but Juan did. Juan hurried her toward the rear of the cave to escape the torrent of water front expressions, none of them polite.

"Wait a moment. We will need a torch," Juan told her, when they had reached what seemed a blank wall at the far end of the rock-lined cave. And he hurried back and got a length of driftwood that he thrust into the flames until the end caught fire.

"Now we can go, if you think you are strong enough to do some climbing."

"I'm okay," Janet assured him, but her teeth were starting to chatter again with another chill. "Let's go!"

It was a good thirty feet to the tall slab of rock that

seemed to be the rear wall of the cave. But as Juan and Janet approached it, the torchlight showed that there was a space beyond the slab. The end of the cave was not the blank wall Janet had expected. Instead, there was a small, low hole about three feet high.

"Through here," Juan bent low, holding the torch ahead of him. "It's only a little way." He went on in.

Janet hesitated, but she could hear Juan's footsteps and when she bent and peered through the hole in the wall, she could see the light of the torch getting farther away all the time. "Guess I'd better go," she decided. She didn't want to be in the cave alone, even with the amusing El Capitan Pedro for company.

She bent over and hurried through the passageway after Juan. And when she came out, she was in a tall dark room apparently hollowed out of the hill.

"Where are we?" she whispered, awed.

"In the hill right behind the rear yard of the ranch house," Juan told her. He held the torch high so she could look around. "This was a place where the ancient Indians hid from the pirates from Spain."

"Br-r-r!" Janet shivered as she looked around the circular, dirt-walled room. "Did the pirates find them?"

Juan grinned. "I think not. There would be skeletons, in that case. But there were only a few pieces of pottery, very old, and the fire pit where they cooked."

"How did *you* find all this?" Janet was wide-eyed.

"I was spearfishing last year, and found the cave as I swam past. No one else knows of it." He smiled proudly, but his expression became stern a moment later. "Except you, Miss Janet. And I have your word not to tell anyone!"

"Honest!" Janet reassured him. And as he relaxed again, she asked pertly, "And how do we get out of *here?*"

He pointed to the opposite wall, which looked solid. "Through there."

As Janet stood open-mouthed, watching him, he crossed over, still carrying the torch, and put his hand on one side of a tall rock that seemed imbedded in the dirt wall. With almost no pressure, he swung the rock around, until it was standing out at right angles to the wall. "Come and look!" he called to Janet.

She went eagerly, and saw that there was a second round room beyond, but a very small one this time. And a flight of wooden steps led up from the floor and became a winding stairway. The steps were hand cut, very old, with the axe-marks still plain on them.

"Do you feel like climbing?" Juan asked. "It is rather steep. We could go slowly."

"I'm the best climber in the whole Lennon family!" Janet told him, with a flash of her usual spirit. "I'll be right on your heels."

So they started up, and even after the stairs finished and the rest of the way was by steps cut into rocks, Janet never faltered, but kept gamely close to her guide.

At last there was daylight ahead and above. Juan thrust his torch into the damp earth of the passageway to extinguish it, and went on.

A few feet from the top, he stopped Janet. "Remember, it was John Smith, a stranger, who rescued you, and he went away at once when you were safe."

"Okay. I guess I owe you that for saving my life, but I wish you'd let my daddy talk to you. I'm sure he could help you get out of trouble, whatever it is. He's real smart, and he knows a lot of people."

"No. I will be all right when Bernardo returns," Juan said stubbornly. "I must keep out of sight till then."

"Can I bring you something to eat? I'll leave it where you can get it. Maybe under the old olive tree in the kitchen yard? We're having chocolate layer cake for dinner and there should be a nice hunk left!"

Juan's eyes gleamed hungrily, but he quickly shook his head. "No, please. The old man might see me. Besides, I have already taken too much of your food—the cookies and other things."

"Hey! Then it was you who left the money? Gosh, you didn't have to do that! We've got lots."

"I try to pay for what I use," Juan said with dignity. "But it was far too little."

"Well, you've paid plenty by saving my life," Janet reminded him. "You better come and get that stuff tonight."

Juan smiled. "Perhaps. But now, you had better hurry to your sisters, before they alarm your family about you."

"Yeah!" Janet hadn't thought of that. And when Juan led her up and out onto the top of the hill, she said a hasty good-by. Then she hurried down the hillside along a cattle trail that Juan pointed out to her as it twisted back and forth through the thick chaparral that covered the hill.

Juan crouched on the brow of the hill and watched till she reached the foot of the slope and began running through the tall weeds to the rear gate. She opened it and as she started into the rear yard, she looked back up at the top of the hill. And even though she could not see Juan at all, she waved cautiously before she closed the gate behind her and walked quickly toward the kitchen door.

Juan watched her go, and then he turned away and went back to the mouth of the chimneylike opening they had ascended. The storm was gone now, but the sandy ground was still damp, and showed their footprints clearly.

Juan took a switch from a chaparral bush and carefully smoothed the ground. And before he went down to his cave again, he had destroyed all signs that there was a hidden entrance there.

Now, if he could depend on the little girl's promise, he would still be safe. And surely Bernardo would be coming back from his trip to Mexico soon, and Chris Lugo's false charge against him would be dismissed. He felt sure that Lugo would drop the charge when Bernardo sternly demanded an accounting of the money he had left with his cousin for Juan's care.

None of her three sisters was in the kitchen as Janet quietly pushed open the back door and went in. She kept on to the hallway, and finally she heard voices in the big living room. The door was slightly ajar, and she tiptoed up to it and listened. Someone was sobbing hard. It sounded like Kathy.

And then she heard Deedee's voice say brokenly, "I suppose there's no use putting it off any longer. One of us has to phone Mom and Daddy and tell them. And I guess it's up to me."

Janet peeked in. Kathy was crying, with her face in her hands, her long hair streaming down wetly on her shoulders. Peggy looked as drenched as Kathy did, but she was trying to be brave, and had her arm over Kathy's shoulders, her own face wet and her voice shaky as she told Kathy, "It's no use crying so hard, Kathy. It won't bring her back. We've got to be brave now."

Dianne turned and started toward the door, her shoulders drooping. And then she saw Janet grinning at her from the doorway. She gave a gasp and staggered as if she were going to faint, staring wide-eyed at Janet.

"Hi!" Janet said, "here I am!"

11

Secrets

For an instant, the three girls stared at Janet, as she smiled saucily at them from the doorway of the living room. They couldn't believe their eyes.

Then, with an exclamation of joy and relief, Dianne ran to her with outstretched arms and hugged her wildly, while Peggy and Kathy rushed up to try and hug her at the same time, all babbling excited, hysterical questions.

Janet was really enjoying herself, being the center of attention, until Dianne, taking hold of herself, stepped back suddenly and said, "Girls! Please! Let's hear what happened! Janet, how did you get out of that horrible rip tide? The last thing we knew, you had been swept away out of sight!"

Janet nodded solemnly. "I tried to swim, but the tide upset me and rubbed my nose in the sand. And when I came up for air, I wasn't in our cove at all!" She giggled a little. "And a nice boy who was swimming there came along and helped me get ashore. And when I felt all right, why, I just came on home."

"A boy? Who was he? Where is he now?" Dianne asked quickly. "We must thank him."

"He's gone," Janet told her. "I guess he didn't want a fuss to be made over him."

"But who was he?" Peggy insisted.

"Well, he said I could call him 'John Smith.' "

"That sounds pretty phony to me," Peggy scoffed.

"It's a perfectly good name," Janet snapped.

"Of course it is," Dianne told her, flashing a frown at Peggy. "And when Daddy gets here Saturday, he'll find your rescuer and give him a nice reward."

"That'll be fine," Janet said meekly.

"And now we're all going to get out of our wet clothes and try to look like human beings again," Dianne said cheerfully. "And I think you'd better rest in bed this afternoon, or you might catch cold."

Janet was remarkably willing to follow orders for once, and let herself be escorted upstairs and petted and coddled by her happy sisters.

And a little later, as Ben Taggart came into the kitchen with a long face, to ask the girls if they had called the authorities to report their sister's drowning, he was astounded to see all three of them smiling and happy as they gathered to plan dinner.

"She's home, safe and sound!" Peggy laughed, when he stood with dropped jaw in the doorway.

"But how—how did she get back to shore through them high waves?" Taggart was relieved but puzzled.

"Some boy helped her, she says," Kathy explained happily.

"A boy? Here?" Taggart's eyes narrowed. "I ain't seen any boy around here. What's his name?"

"John. John Smith. Isn't that a silly name?" Kathy laughed. "But that's what he told her, anyhow! Maybe he was afraid if he told her his right name, she'd think she had to marry him because he saved her life!" She and Peggy burst into peals of laughter at the silly thought.

But Ben Taggart only smiled grimly. There was one boy it could be—and he was a boy it might be dangerous for them to get acquainted with! He didn't believe Lugo's word that the runaway Juan knew nothing about the plans of Luis Duran and Chris Lugo. Suppose he told the girls?

At that moment, Ben Taggart made up his mind that if he could find that runaway boy, he would catch him and turn him over to Chris Lugo. That would take care of him.

But he didn't intend to let the girls know what he had in mind. He hadn't been able to scare them into leaving, so far, but he would keep trying till the last minute. And then if he failed, he would just have to find some way to keep them indoors till the yacht had finished its business ashore and was on its way south.

He made a quick try, as he started out the back door. "It's a good idea not to get too friendly with strangers, girls. That 'John Smith,' now, he might be a real bad one."

"He saved my life! He's nice!" Janet had come into the kitchen wrapped in a blanket and was frowning angrily at the old man. "I like him!"

"Just the same," he insisted gloomily, "he might cut your throats for a silver dollar! There's been things like that happened on other places so far from town!" He went out, shaking his head and slamming the door after him.

"Ugh!" Peggy shivered. "He certainly can paint pretty pictures, can't he? He makes chills run down my spine!"

"He's a silly old—" Janet began indignantly, but Dianne interrupted her hastily.

"That'll do, Jan! I'm sure Mr. Taggart means his advice for our good. Run up and get your clothes on if you feel rested enough to sit up for dinner." And she pointed sternly toward the door.

Janet hesitated, pouting, but finally she started out, holding the blanket around her and tossing her head indignantly. She stopped in the doorway to look back at them. "I wouldn't have almost drowned if that mean old character hadn't told me I could catch a big fish out on those rocks! I bet he knew the waves were going to get high!" Then she marched out.

The girls looked at each other with troubled expressions, but after a moment they relaxed and Peggy grinned.

"I don't believe he'd want to get rid of us that badly," she laughed. "Janet has a good imagination!"

"Just the same," Kathy said uneasily, "I think we should tell Daddy about it when he gets here Saturday morning."

They were all worn out by the strain of the day, so it wasn't long after dinner when all the girls went to their rooms to bed.

But Janet only waited a few minutes after the lights were out, before she stole downstairs, still fully dressed, and groped her way along the lower hall to the kitchen.

The light of an almost full moon was shining into the room as she moved noiselessly about, cutting a generous slice of the chocolate cake and packing it into a little basket along with one of her precious candy bars and some peanuts. As a last touch, she added a bottle of soda pop from the refrigerator and, after some thought, a couple of slices of bread. The basket now being quite full, she opened the outside door, and started out with it.

But on the doorstep, she stopped suddenly and shrank back into the shadow, frightened. Someone was moving about out there with a flashlight. And now, whoever it was seemed to be coming toward the back door.

In a panic, Janet slipped inside the kitchen again and closed the door. She stood rigid in the dark room, listening to the footsteps outside and seeing the light flash past the windows a couple of times. Old Taggart's warning against the runaway boy came back to her with terrifying suddenness, but she was too frightened to move.

Then she heard Ben Taggart's rasping cough, and a second later, his door closed. She almost dropped the basket of food, in her relief. "Boy! Am I glad he didn't run into me out there!" she told herself. "I hope he stays in his room the rest of the night!"

She waited a few minutes, and then stole out and left the basket under the old olive tree. She would have liked to wait around and see if Juan came for it, but it was too risky. Old Mister Gloom might decide to do some more patrolling.

She hurried up to her room and started to undress in the dark. Suddenly she heard light footsteps in the hall, and saw a line of light under her door. Somebody was coming in!

She made a leap into bed and under the covers, and half a minute later, Dianne came in with a flashlight. Janet summoned up a gentle snore and kept her eyes tight closed, while Dianne felt her forehead to see if she had a temperature after her adventure of the day.

Satisfied that Janet had no fever, Dianne tucked the covers around her, kissed her gently on the cheek, and tiptoed out, closing the door quietly behind her.

"Wow!" Janet sat up in bed. "I just made it!" And after she had finished undressing, she popped back into bed and was asleep in a minute.

But several hours later, when the first streaks of dawn lightened the sky, she awoke suddenly and sat up in bed. "Okay, I'm getting up!" she said drowsily. Then as her

eyes opened wider, she saw that it was still almost dark outside. "I guess I dreamed Kathy was calling me to get up," she thought sleepily. Then she saw what had awakened her.

It was El Capitan Pedro, perched on her window sill, fluttering his wings, and cocking his head as he looked at her.

"Why, hello, Capitan!" she said softly.

The mynah answered in an excellent imitation of Juan's voice. *"Muchas gracias, señorita! Muchas gracias!"* Then it flew off into the darkness.

Janet bounced out of bed and ran to the window, but it was too dark for her to see Juan, if he was there. So she went back to bed feeling happy. "That's a cute way to say thanks! I wish I could tell Deedee and the others! But Juan said not to, so I guess I won't."

Janet wasn't the only one who heard a voice that early dawn. Ben Taggart heard it too. But the voice he heard was Chris Lugo's, at first, and then it was young Juan Lopez's, and then something like Bernardo Lopez's deep tones as he called brisk orders to his fishermen on the tuna clipper.

So Ben knew that it was the boy Juan's pet bird that was flying about outside his window. That meant that Juan himself must be somewhere near.

Before he dropped off to sleep again, Taggart made up his mind to search the ranch in the morning. If the boy should still be there, he would capture him for Chris Lugo, who would know how to keep the runaway from blabbing any secrets he might have overheard.

So very early in the morning, before the girls were stirring, he started out, shotgun in hand, to hunt for Juan Lopez who called himself John Smith.

He found prints of bare feet in the ranch yard, but lost the trail in the wild thicket of chaparral beyond the rear gate. Grimly, he kept on searching.

When Janet awoke a little later, she dressed in her jeans and sweater and hurried out to see if Juan had left the empty basket.

The basket was there, under the olive tree, but now it had a mysterious little bundle of seaweed in it, still damp from the sea. When she looked under the seaweed, she was delighted to discover that Juan had left her a small collection of delicate little sea shells lying in a bed of seaweed.

She ran into the kitchen with them, to examine them admiringly out of range of Taggart's eye if he should be prowling around.

"Where did you find those?" Peggy's voice came suddenly behind her.

"Uh—out in the back yard," Janet replied truthfully.

"Where'd the seaweed come from? It's still damp!" Kathy was there, too, in her pet bathrobe. She fingered the seaweed gingerly.

"From the water, I guess," Janet answered airily, and gathered up her sea shells and fled to her room before they could ask any more leading questions.

But Dianne, hearing about it, was worried. "That boy who calls himself John Smith probably gave them to her. I don't want her to be seeing him unless one of us is around, even if he did save her life. As Mr. Taggart says, there's no telling who or what he is."

"He's probably some local kid," Peggy guessed. "He'll probably hang around till Daddy gets here, and then expect a reward."

"What's wrong about that?" Kathy asked quietly. "He certainly rates it, no matter who he is."

They agreed, but they were still uneasy. "I don't see why he doesn't come talk to us," Dianne said, frowning. "It seems funny."

But a minute later, she almost forgot about the mysterious

John Smith, when she discovered that several items of food had been taken, including the big hunk of chocolate cake.

"Bet it was Mr. Taggart who helped himself," Peggy guessed laughingly. "He must be beginning to think of himself as one of the family!"

"That's better than trying to scare us off with bad luck stories and fake animal screams!" Kathy agreed.

"He'll quit all that once he gets used to having all the family around. He'll be meek as a lamb when Nana gets through with him!" Dianne laughed confidently. "And he'll miss us when we leave!"

But Taggart, grimly intent on running down the missing Lopez boy, wasn't looking that far ahead just then. He had been out to the storage cabin, examining the ground for tracks of the boy's bare feet, but the only prints he could find were his own. If the boy had been here snooping around, the rain yesterday had washed out his footprints.

The cabin door was locked, as Taggart had left it when he stowed away the last two cases that Lugo had entrusted to him, and the window was still boarded up and showed no signs of tampering.

He breathed easy for the first time all morning. Maybe the boy was gone. He hoped so. But he climbed the next hill, just the same, and stopped on a cliff overlooking the big cove where the yacht was to put in when it came. There was a pretty beach in that cove, but it was almost impossible to climb down to it, so no one ever went there.

Taggart knew a way down to the beach, and so did Lugo. It was that secret little path on which the men from the ship would come to the storage cabin and get the valuable cargo hidden there. But the path, winding as crazily as any cow path in those hills, had been allowed to grow over with weeds and brush. Unless one knew where to look, it was no different from the rest of the rugged hillside where wild goats roamed and the long-strayed cattle of the deserted ranch lived a free life.

The cove was empty now, but some time today, if the message he had picked up from the *Starlight* still held, the big yacht would be at anchor there.

12 *The Yacht*

Ben Taggart made his way down the narrow path on the hill whose windward side was the cliff overlooking Big Cove. Between the cove hill and the ranch there was only one more hill, the one that overlooked the rear yard of the ranch.

He had seen the prints of bare feet a couple of times so far today, but there had been no other trace of the missing Juan Lopez. He was tired of climbing about and getting more angry against the boy every minute. He plodded along the path doggedly, looking about sharply from time to time.

He kept his shotgun ready. There were wild boars roaming the chaparral on this almost uninhabited side of the large island, and it was a matter of record that they had been known to attack a man without warning. They were mean customers to run into, with their tusks and their evil tempers.

But he failed to see one, though he sighted a dozen or so of the half-wild cattle in a group near the trail. He moved cautiously so he wouldn't disturb them. They weren't as dangerous as the boars, but they were apt to charge a man who was afoot, especially when there were calves in the bunch, as there were now.

He was just about to cross the little valley and start up the last hill, when he heard voices from the other side of the hill. He recognized Janet's voice at once.

There was a small clump of low-growing oaks a few yards away, and he hurried to cover there. He hoped that Janet's companion would be the boy Juan. He would pounce on him unexpectedly, and bundle him off to Holiday Town as a wanted thief.

But when Janet appeared at the top of the hill, the old man was disappointed to see that it was Peggy who was with her. And having hidden himself, he would have to stay hidden till they had passed—or explain. And an explanation of his search for the Lopez boy would give Janet a chance to warn him! So he crouched there, waiting for them to pass.

Janet's voice carried clearly to him. "I don't see why you had to tag along with me. I only wanted to come up and look at the view!"

"And I'd much rather have finished writing my letter!"

"Well, why didn't you, then?"

"Because after your cute stunt yesterday, scaring all of us, Dianne says you're not to go away from the house alone again until the folks get here tomorrow! And of course, Kathy was waiting for a phone call, as usual. So I was the goat!" She was only half in earnest.

"Har!" Janet snorted. "Okay, if you're going to come along, let's see you do it!" And without any further warning, she turned and started running at top speed down the hill toward the little valley where the caretaker was hiding.

"Wait, you little demon! You'll trip and break a leg! Then we'll have to shoot you!" Peggy called after her laughingly. But Janet kept going, her pony tail hair-do flying out behind her. And after an exasperated moment, Peggy took off to catch up to her.

And as Peggy ran, she called out, "Bet a soda I can beat you to the top of the hill, smarty pants!"

And she had practically caught up with her shorter-legged sister by the time they reached the little valley. "Still want to race to the top?" she challenged. "Give up?"

Janet made a face back at her and started up the hill, coming within a few feet of Ben Taggart, who held his breath, expecting any moment to be discovered. But Janet went right on past, and a moment later Peggy went by too. They were both breathing hard, but laughing at the same time. A few feet beyond his hiding place, Peggy caught up with Janet, and they both stopped to catch their breath, holding each other up weakly.

"I won!" Peggy panted. "Now you owe me a soda when we get to Holiday Town tomorrow to meet the folks!"

"Okay!" Janet grinned at her, still puffing, "but you'll have to lend me the price! I've already spent my next month's allowance!"

"I knew I'd get gypped one way or the other!" Peggy laughed, as they threw themselves flat on the edge of the cliff, and looked down admiringly at the pretty half-moon beach. The water looked peaceful from up there, with no sign of a rip tide with its slanting waves.

"Look at those quiet little waves coming in! Now, why can't our cove be like this one?" Peggy complained.

Janet shivered. "I bet it isn't always so calm here. Our cove looks peaceful, too, when there isn't a storm." She glanced out toward the drifting clouds suspiciously, but they were white and fleecy today, without a hint of danger.

Suddenly she sat up straight. "Hey, look! Coming around the point! A gorgeous big white yacht!"

Peggy looked. "I wish we'd brought along a camera!" she said regretfully. "That's a stunning picture. Wonder whose it is?"

"Some millionaire, I bet! It's big enough to go all around the world, isn't it?" Janet was wistful. "Lucky guy, whoever he is!"

"It's turning to come into this cove!" Peggy exclaimed excitedly.

The great white yacht, sleek and gleaming, its brasswork shining in the sun and its one smokestack sending out a thin trail of smoke, was indeed heading into the half-moon cove.

They hung their heads over the edge of the cliff to watch, stretched out on the grass. They could see the sudden activity on the deck of the yacht, as the smokestack gave one last puff and the big yacht drifted in to an anchorage a safe distance from shore. An anchor went over the side, its chain rattling loudly.

"Wonder how much it costs to run—" Janet stopped

speaking abruptly and stared down at the yacht. "Look at those men coming out of the rear cabin. They're all dressed like pirates!"

Peggy studied them a moment, and then said disappointedly, "Wouldn't you know, it's just a movie company on location! A fine lot of millionaires!"

Janet was disappointed too. Movie-making was no novelty to the Lennon girls. They had lived in the midst of it all their lives, only a short distance from several big studios. Besides which, they had spent many hours in front of a camera themselves, for their television show.

"Still," Janet said thoughtfully, "it might be fun to go down and watch them act!"

But Peggy shook her head. "How are you going to get down there off this cliff? Sprout wings?"

So Janet contented herself for a few minutes with watching the "pirates" lower a small boat, not very expertly. "I don't see any cameras or lights or reflectors," she said, with a puzzled frown. "I guess they're not going to shoot any scenes right away."

"Two of the pirates are getting into the little boat," Peggy said after a few moments. "They're coming ashore."

Ben Taggart had heard the anchor chain drop, and he

had left his hiding place on the hillside to take a quick look at the big yacht. He could hear the girls talking on the cliff above. He hoped fervently that they would stay where they were till he could get down to the beach and warn Luis Duran and the bearded man who was with him in the small boat, that there was danger of their movements being watched.

Once he had warned them, he thought, they could take the yacht out of the cove again, and return after dark.

He started down the winding cattle trail, but as he passed below the cliff edge that overhung it, he could hear Janet declare firmly, "I'm going down to the beach and watch what they do. I hope they stage a big fight. Or dig up a buried treasure chest! It's better than just sitting here look-ing at scenery!"

"Oh, bother! Why can't you settle down for five whole minutes some time? Besides, there probably is no way to get down from here!"

"We crossed a cattle trail coming up. I'm going to see where it leads to! Bet it goes to the beach!"

Ben Taggart stopped where he was. "I've got to stop her somehow," he thought in a panic. "But how?"

Then he thought of the wild cattle grazing close to the

trail. He gripped his shotgun and turned on the narrow path.

Around the corner of the hill, Janet was climbing down toward the cattle trail. Above her, Peggy was arguing, "Forget it, Jan! Come back here!" But when Janet ignored her order, Peggy gave up and followed her sister down to the trail.

"See? It's been used lately. I can see a boot print!" Janet said eagerly. "Come on!"

"Please, Janet! Daddy will be furious if we talk to strangers! Let's forget it and go back to the house. It's almost lunch time, anyhow."

"Chicken!" Janet said witheringly. "I just want to watch a few minutes. Come along!"

But they hadn't gone more than twenty feet along the narrow, indistinct trail on the hillside, when they heard two shots, and a moment later, the bellowing of cattle. They looked at each other, startled.

"Shots! They've started to take a scene already! Let's hurry and watch!" Janet started to run. Peggy grabbed her arm and held her.

"Wait! Listen!" Peggy was puzzled only a moment, then she knew! The thunder of pounding hoofs and the bellowing and squealing of frightened cattle were getting closer. "Let's get out of here, fast!"

Janet had no time to question, as Peggy pulled her back along the trail with her. Soon she was running with Peggy, as the meaning of the sounds came to her also.

They had gone only a few feet when Peggy cast a quick look behind her, and saw the first of the running cattle coming around the corner of the narrow trail. It was a big, crossbred bull with long pointed horns. His head was lowered and he was bellowing angrily as he ran. She could see, in the cloud of dust behind him, the moving backs of more cattle, who squealed and snorted as they ran blindly after their leader.

Peggy knew in a flash that she and Janet could not outrun the terrified animals. But to stay on that narrow trail meant they would certainly be trampled to death!

There were scrub oaks on the hillside. Peggy grabbed for a sturdy one, and pulled at it. It held.

"Quick, grab this and pull yourself up!" she ordered, giving Janet a boost. Janet grasped the bush with both hands and pulled herself up off the trail, flattening her body against the hillside only a few inches above the level of the backs of the running cattle.

The moment that Peggy saw Janet was high enough to be safe, she yelled, "Hang on!" and grasped another bush close by and pulled herself clear, only half a second before the giant bull rushed by with his dozen followers.

The dust billowed around the two girls as they clung to the sturdy bushes on the hillside, and for a minute or two they couldn't even see each other. Then as the sea breeze blew the dust away, Janet turned anxious eyes in search of her sister, and was relieved to see her safe.

"Okay, kid?" Peggy called to her, and Janet had to puff out a mouthful of dust before she could answer.

"Is it safe to let go?" Janet queried shakily.

Peggy listened for stragglers a moment, then dropped lightly to the trail and stood weakly leaning against the hillside. "I guess we've had 'em all," she told Janet. "How about home sweet home before something else happens?"

And for once, Janet didn't object. She was willing to forget her interest in the "movie company" and get back to the ranch house for a much-needed shower!

They started back more slowly than usual, both still shaken by their narrow escape.

And when they had gotten down to the valley, they lingered a moment before they started to climb the last hill that lay between themselves and the ranch.

Peggy looked back at the cattle trail where they had nearly met with disaster. "We'll stay off that thing from now on," she said grimly. Then she stared. Old Taggart was coming around the bend in the trail, carrying his shotgun. "Look! Mr. Taggart must have fired those shots!"

"Wonder what he was hunting?" Janet said. Then, cupping her hands around her mouth, she called up to the old man, "Hey!"

Ben Taggart had come to see what had happened to the two girls. There had been no sign of them as he scanned the trail, and he had just decided that they had been swept off the narrow path by the stampede, when he heard Janet's yell from below. He stared down at them, amazed.

"Was that you shooting?" Janet yelled. "You started a stampede!"

"Not me, Miss Janet," he called back promptly, "never fired a shot all day! But I heard them shots. Probably strangers doin' some huntin'. Better run on home before you get hurt."

"We're going right now!" Peggy yelled to him, and she took her young sister by the arm and started up the last hill with her.

Old Ben looked after them with narrowed eyes. It wasn't that he wanted to hurt them real bad, he thought, but if they had got trampled a little, maybe it would have been better. Then maybe they would have decided it was an unlucky place and got out before things started happening that they might get mixed up in and be sorry.

He sighed heavily, and went on back to the cattle trail. After some climbing back and forth, he got down to the beach and met the two men in their pirate costumes.

"You've got to put off movin' that stuff out of the cabin," he urged Luis Duran.

But the smooth-spoken leader of the men shook his head firmly. "It is not possible, my friend. Tomorrow morning my men come ashore to get the cargo. It will be very bad for these people if they cross our path. And for you it will be worse, old man."

And Ben Taggart knew, finally, that he was dealing with desperate men who would sacrifice him as soon as they would anyone else.

He listened meekly while the arrogant Duran gave him orders, and even though he resented the orders, he knew he would carry them out to the letter. He had no other choice. He was in too deep.

13   *A Helping Hand*

"I'm glad it's all downhill from here!" Peggy and Janet had paused on the hill overlooking the rear yard of the ranch.

"Me, too. I'm shaky!" Janet sat down on a rock to rest a few minutes.

"Look who's coming!" Peggy pointed down toward the yard. Kathy was coming up the hill. "Hey!" she called down to her.

Kathy looked up and waved. "You all right? Deedee's been worrying."

"Sure! We're fine! Come on up and look at the view!" Janet called impishly. She knew Kathy wasn't the hiking type if she could side-step it. "It's gorgeous!"

Kathy hesitated. They could see that she was trying to think of an excuse to bypass the extra effort. But after a moment, she gave in, and started up toward them.

They watched her climb as they rested, and when she reached the top and looked around, they giggled as she said indignantly, "Why, you can't see anything but a lot of ocean from here! Where's the view?"

"Back there on the next hill! Want to go look?" Janet's eyes twinkled, and she giggled again at Kathy's disgusted expression. "There's a big yacht. Want to see it?"

"I should say not! And I think you're both mean to make me climb all this way for nothing!" She was ready to start down again at once, but she stopped before she had gone ten steps. "What on earth is that?"

They heard it, too, then. It was a snorting and puffing, mixed with a deep growling. And it was only a few yards away in the brush.

But Janet heard something else. And so did Peggy. It was a deep voice coming from that brush, and it was calling, "*Adelante! Vamos!*" over and over.

"The voice!" Peggy exclaimed, astonished.

But Janet knew who it was. And from the sounds that came over the excited Capitan Pedro's voice, she knew something was going on. "Juan!" she shouted, grabbing up a dry branch to use as a weapon, and running through the chaparral toward the sounds of conflict. "I'm coming!"

Her sisters looked at each other amazed. "Janet! What is it?" Kathy called, frightened. "Come back!"

But Peggy lost no time running after Janet, who had already disappeared into the thicket, and a moment later, Kathy picked up a small rock and valiantly followed them.

As Janet crashed through the brush, she saw Juan cornered and trying to defend himself against the rushes of a tusked boar. She stopped, staring, and Juan saw her.

"Run, Miss Janet!" he called. "Get away!" and he struck at the boar with a stick as it made a short run toward him and then veered off, growling and snorting.

But Janet wasn't running. Instead, she threw the branch of deadwood at the animal, and hit it. Instantly, it turned away from its intended victim, and charged at Janet. She gave a little shriek and ducked behind a rock, and the animal stopped, pawing the ground and snorting, getting ready for another charge.

By that time, Peggy and Kathy were there, and as Peggy faced the wild animal, yelling and waving her arms, Kathy let fly with her chunk of rock, and hit the boar fairly on the snout, just as it started to charge.

The animal gave a pained grunt, stopped, looked

bewildered, and gave ground as all three girls yelled and waved their arms at it threateningly. And when Juan landed a strong wallop with his stick on its hindquarters, the boar suddenly turned tail and crashed off into the bushes.

They stood listening a moment, as the sounds of its grunting and snorting died away and the crashing of brush became farther and farther distant.

Janet was the first to recover. She grinned at Juan. "Hi, John Smith!" she said.

Juan made a funny little bow, and looked rather shyly at the two older girls. "Thank you, Miss Janet. I am lucky that you came along. My little stick wasn't scaring that boar a bit!"

"Now we're even!" she laughed. And then, seeing Kathy and Peggy staring at Juan, she added hastily, "Peg, Kathy, this is Juan! I mean John Smith. He's the one who pulled me out of the rip tide!"

"So we gathered!" Peggy said dryly, looking Juan over keenly, sizing him up.

But Kathy smiled and went to Juan holding out her hand. "We're very grateful for what you did."

Juan took her outstretched hand and beamed into her smiling face. It was quite obvious that he had been smitten at first sight! "It was nothing, Miss Kathy," he said modestly. "I just happened to see her in the waves and brought her to shore." They stood smiling at each other.

Peggy looked at Janet, and raised one eyebrow. Janet looked back, and raised an answering one. They had seen others affected that way by Kathy.

"If you hadn't thrown that rock at the boar," Juan told Kathy earnestly, "someone might have been hurt."

Janet wrinkled her nose at Peggy, and Peggy coughed gently as a reminder that they were still around.

Kathy knew that signal, and blushed. "Oh, it was just a lucky throw!" she told him hastily.

And at that moment, El Capitan Pedro swooped in and perched on Juan's shoulder, saying, in Kathy's voice, "Lucky throw! Lucky throw!"

And in the laughter that followed, from all four, Kathy's momentary embarrassment was forgotten.

But Janet was a little miffed, as she saw Juan making friends with her sisters. He was so fussy about her telling anyone she had seen him! And yet here he was, sitting down on a log between Peggy and Kathy, and telling them how smart Capitan Pedro was and how his father Bernardo had bought him for him last year.

And a few minutes later, under their friendly questioning, Juan was telling them all about his father's having gone to Mexico and leaving him in the care of his distant cousin, Chris Lugo. And how he had run away after a bad beating by his cousin, and was now "wanted" by the police for a theft that he had not committed.

At first, Janet listened with a pout, feeling hurt that he was so ready to confide in the older girls. But as Juan went on with his story, she forgot to be jealous and asked him more questions than they did.

When he had finished answering and explaining, Peggy said promptly, "I think we should tell Daddy all about it when he gets here tomorrow. I'm sure he can help you get things straightened out."

"The little one," he smiled at Janet, "thought so too. And perhaps it would be a good idea. Except that Ben Taggart is a friend of my cousin, and would swear to your father that I am a bad one, a thief. Then they would take me back to Lugo, and there would be more beatings."

They all had long faces at that, until Janet said suddenly, "Old Mister Gloom doesn't have to know you're here! I'll bring Daddy out to look at the scenery tomorrow afternoon. And you can be waiting—*you know where!*" She made mysterious gestures toward the hidden entrance to the chimneylike passage down to the Indian caves.

"What on earth are you talking about?" Peggy demanded. She looked where Janet was pointing but all she could see was a thick growth of chaparral.

"Never mind," Janet said with a smug smile. "We know, don't we, Juan?"

Juan nodded but made no explanation. He was suddenly sneezing. "Excuse me," he smiled. "The cave is a little damp when the sea mist rolls in along toward morning."

"You shouldn't sleep there," Peggy told him in her elder-sister voice. "You'll get pneumonia."

"Pneumonia," mimicked the mynah. "No, no, no!" And he shook his wings.

Juan smiled ruefully. "El Capitan Pedro sides with you. But where else would I be safe?"

Kathy spoke quickly. "There's a storage cabin back here somewhere. Mr. Taggart took some groceries out to it Wednesday. I bet it would be just the place for you, nice and dry and warm."

"And right where he could find me!" Juan shook his head, but he smiled gratefully at Kathy. "I'm sorry."

"But it would only be for one night. Tomorrow Daddy

will be here, remember. And once you get a chance to tell him about the beatings, you won't have to hide from old Taggart or anybody else!" Janet urged.

Juan shook his head. "There is still tonight to worry about." He sighed. "Though it would be pleasant to spend one dry night!"

"Look," Janet wrinkled her forehead, "we can snitch the key out of the drawer and bring it to you. And if old droopy whiskers starts to look for it, we can make believe he forgot to put it into the drawer on Wednesday. That should confuse him."

"Unless he has another key, of course!" Peggy reminded her dryly.

"If he had, he wouldn't have had to look for the one in the drawer, Wednesday, Peg," Kathy reminded her. "I think Janet's got a good idea. I'll come with her to be sure she doesn't lose the key on her way here." Kathy smiled sweetly at Juan. "She's sort of careless sometimes."

Janet glared indignantly at her, but before she could remind her that *she* was the one who always lost things, Kathy had said a pretty good-by, and she and Peggy were on their way back to the house. "Well, I like that!" Janet said darkly. But Juan was gazing, slightly moonstruck, after Kathy, and didn't even hear her!

She gave up then, and ran after her sisters. She wasn't going to be left out of it when they told Dianne what was going on.

And Juan, knowing that they would be at least half an hour or more returning, decided that he would go take a look at the storage cabin. He had a hunch that it was back in the trees somewhere. He had seen tire tracks headed that way, since the rain on Monday night. Taggart's old car must have left them. It would be easy to follow them unless the more recent storm had washed them out.

Most of them were gone, but here and there, he saw where the car had passed through the brush and broken small branches from the scrub oaks.

And then, suddenly, he glimpsed the sturdy old log cabin, set back against a hill and all but hidden by a stand of young trees and tall brush.

But his ear caught the sound of men talking, and he stopped in his tracks to listen. The voices were coming from inside the cabin. But he could see no one, though the door was open. There was only one thing to do, stay hidden and just wait. Sooner or later someone would come out of the cabin, and he would see who it was.

The girls were giggling happily as they came across the ranch yard to the kitchen door. It was exciting to be able to help the runaway boy, especially since he had saved Janet's life. They hadn't a doubt in the world that their father could solve all of Juan's problems in a flash.

But Dianne, when she heard the story, was not so sure that they should have promised the runaway any such thing. "How do you know this boy is telling the truth? Maybe he made up the whole story and is really hiding from the police for some serious reason?"

"Not Juan," Janet insisted stubbornly. "He's telling the truth, I know it. And besides, he saved my life. He can't be a criminal!"

"I wish we could be sure," Dianne looked worried. "We owe him a lot for what he did, but—well, why don't I just phone the police station at Holiday Town and sort of ask some questions about him?"

There was a shocked, *"No!"* from all three, and Kathy was almost tearful as she reminded Dianne, "That horrible brute of a cousin, that Lugo or whatever his name is, might find out where Juan is, if we did! We'd be breaking our word to Juan! We told him we wouldn't tell anyone but you and Daddy that we had seen him!"

So Dianne had to give up the idea, though she was not happy about it.

"Has Mr. Taggart been around much today?" Peggy asked.

"Why, no," Dianne shook her head. "Matter of fact, I haven't seen him since early this morning. And that's sort of strange too. He was supposed to fix the washer on this faucet this morning, but he never did come back."

"Goody!" Janet grinned. She darted over to the drawer where the caretaker kept the big key ring. "Hope he stays away all day and all night, the old snoop!" She grabbed the key ring out of the drawer and inspected the labels on the keys.

Kathy was powdering her nose carefully at the kitchen mirror, and fluffing up her pretty curls. Peggy had discovered some coffeecake left from breakfast, and was having an early lunch on it.

Janet's exasperated "Drat it, where's that key?" made all of them look at her.

She held up the keys. "It's not here! I guess he must have taken it with him, wherever he's gone to!"

Kathy grabbed up her sweater and started for the door.

"Where're you going?" Janet demanded.

"To tell Juan he must stay away from the cabin!" Kathy called back over her shoulder, and ran out.

"Wait for me!" Janet was right out after her.

But Peggy calmly smiled and went on eating. "I guess they don't need me!" she laughed. "Looks like there's one messenger too many already."

And Dianne had to agree, with a smile.

But Juan was not waiting at the top of the hill when the two girls breathlessly reached it. And there was no sign that Janet could see that he had walked in the direction of the secret entrance to the sea cave.

She was just as puzzled over where he had gone as Kathy was, but perhaps not so disappointed. *She* hadn't taken a lot of trouble powdering her nose for the second meeting!

But at the moment, Juan had forgotten all about the date with the girls. He was still waiting, crouched in hiding, his eyes fixed on the cabin's open door. And the men whose voices he had heard were still inside.

He played with the idea of trying to sneak up to the side of the cabin where the boarded-up window was and listen. But it would be very risky. Especially if one of the men in there should turn out to be Chris Lugo, as it could very well be!

14   *A Startling Discovery*

Janet and Kathy lingered for a little while at the top of the hill, hoping Juan would return. But Kathy was soon tired of waiting. "Let's get back to the house," she pouted. "I think he was stuffing us with fairy tales, anyhow."

"I don't believe it!" Janet snapped. "He's very sincere! And anyhow, why would he go to the trouble of making up stuff like that?"

"A gag, maybe," Kathy shrugged. Then she frowned with annoyance. "And he seemed like such a nice person! Oh, well, come on, let's give up!"

"Okay, you start. I'll be right along behind you."

So Kathy started down toward the ranch yard again, while Janet scribbled a note on part of a candy bar wrapper, and very carefully stuck it on the spines of a prickly cactus leaf beside the entrance to the cave below. If he had gone down there, he would be sure to see the message when he came up.

Then she followed Kathy down the hill, but she didn't mind too much giving up her wait. She knew she was coming back later, if she could wangle some way to get away from the house. She would bring Juan some food too.

Juan had been crouching in the brush watching the cabin for so long that his legs both had cramps in them when he tried to change his position. He rubbed them hard to restore the circulation, keeping his eye on the cabin door all the while. So far, no one had shown himself.

He could hear snatches of phrases in Spanish, but it didn't sound like Bernardo's Spanish. It had a guttural sound, instead of softness; more, he thought, like a middle European language. He was sure he had heard someone speak with that sort of an accent before, but he couldn't recall when or who it was.

He tried to edge closer and still keep hidden. The window was too well boarded for him to see through it, but he noticed what looked like the end of a packing box sticking out just inside the door.

It *was* a packing box, and there were quite a few in the single-roomed cabin. They were piled high against the walls in stacks nearly reaching the roof beams.

And in there, the two costumed men the girls had seen rowing ashore earlier in the day were watching as Ben Taggart forced open the lid of one of the packing boxes labeled SEWING MACHINE PARTS. There were smaller crates, neatly stacked. Some were labeled, innocently, CANNED PEARS, STRING BEANS, SOLID-PACK TOMATOES. All had been shipped to Chris Lugo, and carried here for Ben Taggart to store where there would be no chance of anyone suspecting what was really inside the boxes.

As the lid came open with a loud squeak, the tall man in the black velvet and gold-sashed pirate costume shoved old Taggart aside, and delved deeply into the contents of the crate. He came up with a machine gun tripod, which he handed to the other man to set up.

Taggart watched greedily as the velvet-clad man brought out parts of the latest model machine gun and gave them to the burly "pirate" whose hamlike hands seemed remarkably skillful putting them together into a shiny sample of a deadly weapon.

"There she is, Mr. Duran!" The "pirate" patted the standing gun proudly. "And a beaut!"

Luis Duran nodded and answered in his strange Spanish,

"Our friends will be glad to pay a top price, if the rest of the fruit is as tasty as this!"

The other two laughed, and Taggart assured him confidently, "Same brand, Lugo says!"

They all laughed at that, and Juan, listening at a distance, wondered what was going on. Once more he heard hammering in there, but he didn't dare get closer to try to hear what the men were saying. Only one sentence came to him, and he recognized the voice of Ben Taggart.

"Suppose our pals don't want to pay what we're askin' for these guns? What then?"

Juan strained his ears for the answer, but he couldn't hear. And he didn't dare get any closer, because just as he was about to try, he heard the sound of a truck approaching. He barely had time to get under cover of the brush again, before Chris Lugo's panel truck came into view, bumping along the weed-grown road toward the cabin.

Taggart appeared instantly in the doorway, his shotgun in the crook of his arm. He saw the truck and waved a greeting. Then he went back into the cabin.

Chris Lugo stopped the truck only a few yards from where Juan lay flattened out behind the bushes. He swung out of the seat and strode toward the cabin.

Juan hardly dared to breathe. Any moment might bring Lugo's heavy hand on his collar.

But the steps went past. Juan hadn't been noticed. And a moment later when he raised his head, he saw Lugo striding toward the cabin, and a tall man in a handsome black pirate outfit was coming out to meet him.

"I've seen him before," Juan thought, "but where?" Then suddenly he remembered. This was the military-looking man whom Lugo had called Don Luis and been very respectful to, one day a few weeks ago. Lugo had quickly sent Juan on an errand in town when the man arrived at the radio shop, but not before Juan had noticed the sharp eye and heard the guttural voice of the stranger.

When Juan had come back from the errand, he recollected, the man had gone. It was his voice that had sounded familiar from inside the cabin.

But what was he doing here, dressed in a pirate costume? And a second man, wearing the same kind of outfit, was coming out now to greet Chris Lugo. Juan knew that one. He was an ex-sailor, a pal of Lugo's, named Carson.

Suddenly he remembered that Janet and Kathy had told him about movie actors in Big Cove. But what was Lugo doing with actors from a movie company? And what did Ben Taggart mean by his question about guns and someone paying for them?

The three men went inside, and for the next few minutes, Juan heard only faint murmurs of conversation. Then, suddenly, they all burst out laughing, and he heard the clink of glasses.

Lugo's voice bellowed out, *"Viva la revolución!"* and the others all laughed loudly and echoed his words.

So that was it! They were all mixed up in a revolution somewhere, and the guns old Taggart had mentioned must be hidden right there in the cabin!

He was tempted to run for the truck and try to get away in it to Holiday Town, to warn the police. But almost at once he remembered that he had no proof of anything wrong against these men. A few words, maybe spoken in fun—that would never convince the police that a runaway like him was telling the truth, if it *was* the truth!

They would think he was spiteful against Chris Lugo for charging him with theft and had made up the story.

The only chance he would have to convince them would be if he could get inside the cabin himself and see what was there. He decided to try it as soon as the men left.

A few minutes later, the four men came out of the cabin,

and Taggart, last to emerge, locked the door after them and dropped the key into his pocket.

Lugo and Don Luis strolled to the panel truck, while Carson fell into step with old Taggart and they headed toward the hill. Juan decided they were probably on their way to Taggart's quarters.

And he suddenly remembered, as the truck with Lugo and Don Luis roared away, that Janet and Kathy were probably waiting for him on top of the hill, with a key to the cabin.

He must get there before old Taggart and Carson did, and warn the girls to go back to the house at once, until he had had time to check what was in the cabin and join them for a discussion about what steps to take next.

He circled the hill, moving fast, and reached the top while the two men were only halfway up. But the girls were not there. He was glad that they weren't, but he also was disappointed at not getting the key.

He wasn't sure just what to do next. The two men were getting closer as they climbed, and he heard Taggart's whining voice. "I don't see why you people want to hang around till morning. Seems to me it would be better to get under way with the stuff tonight!"

"We got a permit to take movies. If we don't take 'em, somebody might ask questions. Why don't you leave the thinkin' to Duran? He's bossin' this caper!" The husky pirate's voice was harsh.

Their words convinced Juan. He had been right! But there was no time to think about it now. He darted for his "chimney" and was scarcely out of sight below the surface, when the two men came past.

He heard a phrase from Taggart, as they went down the hillside toward the ranch yard. " . . . keep your eye out for Lugo's kid cousin . . ." Taggart was saying. Then they went out of hearing.

And when Juan climbed up out of his hiding place again, he saw something he had missed before, in his haste. It was Janet's note, stuck on a spiny cactus leaf. "No key. Wait for me and eats. Janet."

Now he had something else to worry about! Generous, thoughtful little Janet. What if she ran into Taggart and Carson as she came up with food? The old man wouldn't have any trouble guessing that it was for Juan. What would happen then?

All he could do was wait and be on the alert. And as the afternoon sun beat hotly on his back, he watched the two men reach the foot of the hill and stroll across the ranch yard to Taggart's quarters behind the kitchen wing. There was no sign of the girls.

The panel truck was gone. No doubt Lugo and his friend Don Luis were on their way to Holiday Town. Juan hoped they would stay there until he had had time to talk things over with the girls and decide what to do about reporting to the police there.

After the sun had dropped almost beyond the horizon, Juan saw lights go on in the ranch house. "Now they are getting dinner ready," he thought hungrily. "I wish I could risk it. I should like to sit with them at the table." There was nothing to eat in his cave, and he didn't know where to get anything, if Janet didn't bring something as her note promised.

There was a flutter of wings, and El Capitan landed on Juan's shoulder, making soft noises in his throat to greet the boy.

Juan reached up to stroke the sleek black feathers. "At least you are not hungry, my friend!" he said in Spanish to his pet. "It is too bad I do not have wings to fly about to gather fine fat berries for my supper!"

El Capitan gave a tiny squawk and swooped down at

something in a nearby bush. He flew back with it to Juan's shoulder. "What do you have there? A juicy ripe berry, I hope!" Juan held out his palm. "Give it to your starving master!"

But it was no berry. It was a large green caterpillar which Juan quickly dropped to the ground.

Scolding, the mynah swooped down, retrieved his wriggling victim, and flew off to an oak branch to enjoy the unappreciated feast himself.

"Your intentions are good, *amigo,*" Juan told him with a smile, "but your choice of gifts is not so happy!"

In the ranch-house kitchen, the four girls were preparing dinner. Janet and Kathy went about the work silently with long faces. Peggy whistled happily as she scraped carrots and peeled potatoes, and Dianne wore a look of stern determination as she came and went.

Finally, she turned and faced Janet and Kathy. "Stop being silly, both of you. Don't you realize that boy was just making up the whole story about running away from home? He's just getting a rise out of you!"

"But he isn't! I believe him!" Janet bounced angrily on the high stool where she was cutting up salad greens. "And I bet he had an awful good reason for not meeting us like he promised! You just wait and see!"

"He was probably having a good laugh at the silly
Lennons for believing his fairy tales! You'll find out!"
Dianne told her severely.

But for once, all three were siding against her. "Wait till
you meet him," Peggy told her seriously. "You'll see he
isn't fooling."

"We'll let Daddy decide that tomorrow!" Dianne said
firmly. "And let's talk about something else for a change,
please. How about doing a little practicing for tomorrow
night's appearance?"

They weren't too happy about that, at the moment, but
they agreed, and were soon harmonizing on a number.

After a few minutes, Janet sneezed a couple of times.
Dianne felt her forehead anxiously. "I hope you haven't
caught a cold. Perhaps you'd better go lie down awhile."

"Okay," Janet said gloomily, and went to the hall door
dragging her feet.

But the moment the door closed after her, her attitude
changed. She tiptoed hastily to the front door, and let herself out without making a sound.

She went quickly along the side of the house, and ducked
as she passed the lighted kitchen window and Ben Tag-

gart's closed door. His window was closed, and a shade pulled down to the sill kept her from glancing in; but she could hear him laughing and talking to someone, and the other man answering. She didn't try to listen, but hurried on.

She was passing the big olive tree, heading for the hill, when she heard two short trilling whistles, like the sound of a mockingbird. It was the signal she and Juan had arranged.

She stopped and peered toward the tree, but it was too dark to see Juan until he stepped toward her.

"Gosh! I'm glad you came down the hill! I brought you something to eat!" She dug into her pocket and brought out a couple of carrots and a tomato. "It isn't much, but it was all I could grab and hide," she giggled.

"Thank you!" Juan took the vegetables gravely. "They will taste very good. But come over here, where we won't be seen if the old man comes looking! I have something to tell you and your sisters, and to ask your advice."

"Just tell me, and I'll tell them," Janet suggested. "They're kind of busy right now."

So Juan told her hastily about the meeting in the cabin and the snatches of conversation he had heard about guns and revolution. And he told her what he thought it all meant.

But when he had finished his story, he was amazed to see Janet looking at him with an expression of doubt.

"Why do you look like that? Don't you think we should tell this quickly to your elder sisters and get their advice on what I should do?" he demanded, frowning.

But Janet sighed and shook her head. "Uh-uh. Dianne says you've been making up a lot of fairy tales. And this one sure sounds like one!"

"You cannot mean such a thing!" Juan was astounded.

Janet spoke slowly, regretfully. "I'm sorry, Juan. This one is just too much to swallow. I guess Deedee is right. You just invent things to see if we'll believe them." She looked at him pleadingly. "Please—don't fib this time. You've really been kidding, haven't you?"

"No!" Juan was angry and hurt. "Everything I have said is true! I will prove it!"

"I sure hope so," she said earnestly. "But how?"

15 *Captured*

"I will prove to you that everything I have told you is true," Juan assured Janet, as they stood in the shadow of the big olive tree in the ranch yard. "I shall bring you one of those guns of which Ben Taggart spoke. Then you and your sisters will not call me a liar."

"Not a liar, Juan," Janet told him quickly. "You just make up stories, that's all. They're very interesting too. But —how can we believe them? They're so *wild!*"

"You will believe them!" Juan said, with firm conviction and unsmilingly, "when I have brought you proof from the cabin."

"How are you going to get inside it, if it's all locked up and the window boarded, like you say?" Janet asked, with a little smile.

"I shall break through, somehow. Do you know where

I can find a hatchet or something of that sort?"

"Aren't you afraid to make all that noise?" Janet asked, tongue in cheek. "Suppose they hear you?"

"Everyone has left the cabin. How will anyone hear? Where is a hatchet?" Juan persisted.

Janet sighed. He evidently intended to keep up the pretense that he hadn't made up the story. "There's one hanging in the garage," she nodded her head toward the building. "Help yourself!"

"Thank you!" Juan said stiffly. He turned and started to stalk off.

"Juan! Wait!" Janet ran after him. "I'm sorry! I guess I do believe you, really. It's just that Deedee has been saying . . . oh, she just doesn't know you, that's all. *I* know you're telling the truth."

"Thank you!" Juan smiled broadly at her. "I will return soon with a gun of some sort, and then she and the others will all have to believe me!"

"We'll be watching for you!" Janet said as Juan turned away and hurried toward the dark garage.

She waited in the shadows until she saw him come out of the garage again and disappear into the semidarkness at the rear of the yard. There was a small sound of the back gate opening and closing, and then silence.

Janet went back to the house, pausing only a moment to look over her shoulder toward the hill to see if she could catch a glimpse of Juan. But she couldn't see any sign of him. Then, as she started toward the side of the house, someone grabbed her roughly by the shoulder and halted her.

"Where do you think you're going, young fellow?" It was Ben Taggart's voice.

"I'm Janet. Let me go!" she exclaimed, wriggling to escape from his grip.

"Oh, excuse me, Miss Janet!" Ben Taggart let go of her shoulder hastily. "I thought you were that reform school kid that's been prowlin' around, that Lopez!"

The kitchen door flew open, and Dianne and the girls crowded the doorway to look out. "What's going on?" Dianne demanded, her voice unsteady.

"It's all right, Miss Dianne. I thought the little one here was a prowler. I'm sorry!"

"Janet! I thought you were in your room! What are you doing out in the dark alone? Come in here this very instant!"

Janet marched past Taggart and went into the kitchen

past her sisters. "I'd like to talk to you, Deedee!" she said, defiantly glaring at Ben Taggart, who had quietly come in after her, his shotgun still in his left hand.

"I dunno what the young'un was doin' out there in the dark, Miss Dianne, but it ain't safe for her to be runnin' around. My friend that's visitin' me says that kid that pulled her out of the water is wanted for a robbery an' is real dangerous."

"Juan never stole anything!" Janet told him defiantly. "It's that old cousin of his that's bad! And you know all about *that!*" She glared accusingly.

"Janet!" Dianne gasped. "What are you talking about?"

"It's true! Juan heard them! They're taking guns to a revolution somewhere! Hiding them in our cabin!"

Dianne and the other girls exchanged shocked looks. But Ben Taggart broke out in a hearty laugh that made them all stare at him in amazement.

"What's so funny? You just wait! The police will take care of your friends!" Janet stormed.

But Taggart kept on laughing, and when he sobered a moment later, he shook his head grimly and spoke to Dianne with a solemn expression, ignoring Janet. "I don't know what she and that runaway kid are making up such

a story for. I guess it ain't the little lady's fault, except he's got her fooled. The folks she's talkin' about are movie actors, and any guns they've got are old-timers, or just plain fakes!"

Dianne looked baffled and worried, as she turned to Peggy and Kathy for help. "You did see some actors coming ashore, didn't you, Peg?"

"Sure," Peg grinned at Janet. "So did Janet."

"It's just a trick! They're not actors at all!" Janet insisted angrily. "And Juan is going to prove it!"

Taggart shook his head glumly. "Too bad your pa ain't here. He'd give somebody a good spankin'." He moved slowly toward the door, but he stopped in the doorway to look back to Dianne. "My advice is, you better keep her inside. There's no tellin' what that good-for-nothin' Lopez boy will tell her next."

"But why would he make up such stories, Mr. Taggart?" Kathy asked, with a little frown.

"Maybe he wants to be let in, so he can rob the place," Taggart told them. "Better lock up tight tonight."

"I think I'd better telephone the police!" Dianne exclaimed, shivering.

"No need to do that, Miss Dianne. I told them this

afternoon he was hanging around here, and they'll be out first thing tomorrow to pick him up!"

Then he went out, closing the door behind him. But before he went back to his quarters, he took out his pocket knife and bent over in the shrubbery outside the kitchen door, hacking at something. After that, he went quickly to his room and got Carson, and the two of them strode quickly across the rear yard in the direction of the cabin.

Janet was still unconvinced. She had several arguments to bring against the old caretaker. "He didn't tell me I might get drowned out on the rock," she reminded Dianne.

"He didn't think you'd stay there so long, probably," Peggy said. "You were just careless."

"And I still think he started those cattle running and almost had us killed! Nobody else had a gun that we saw!" Janet was almost tearful.

"Now you're being dramatic," Dianne scolded her, "just to shield that boy. How do you know he isn't just what Mr. Taggart says, a real tough character?"

"I just know, that's all!"

"I won't argue any longer with you," Dianne said, with a stern expression. "It's almost time to go to bed, anyhow. So, why don't we just close up the house for the night, and wait to see what happens in the morning?"

"But Juan has gone to get some evidence. He's promised to bring back one of the guns they were talking about, to show the police. That will prove he's telling the truth!" Janet wouldn't give up. "We must wait here."

"When he gets back, *if* he does, he'll have sense enough to knock or ring the bell. You're not going to sit down here and wait. It's probably all a fairy tale, just as Mr. Taggart has been telling us."

She led Janet out of the kitchen with a firm grip on her arm, and the other two followed. They went from one room to the next, upstairs and down, checking to see that every window was locked. They kept together as they went about it, all of them just a little nervous and not nearly so brave as they pretended.

Out at the cabin, Juan was working the boards loose on the window, using the hatchet to pry them apart. He tried to be quiet, and glanced about every now and then to make sure he was alone. Everything seemed quiet, but suddenly without warning, a heavy hand was clapped across his mouth and he was thrown roughly to the ground.

He lay there dazed for a few seconds, and then was dragged to his feet by Carson and led, stumbling, to the door which Ben Taggart had opened by that time.

Once inside, the two men proceeded to tie up the boy, in spite of his struggles. They left him trussed up and helpless on the dirt floor.

"Maybe we ought to gag him too," Carson suggested.

"What's the use? If he choked, we'd be in hot water for sure! Come on, let's lock up and get goin'. We've got to find Don Luis an' Lugo real fast, now."

"Hope you got those Lennon kids calmed down!" Carson said, with a heavy frown.

The old man chuckled. "Don't worry yourself! They're put for the night. I know how to handle young'uns. They won't give us any trouble!"

So they went out and left Juan in the darkness, tied hand and foot, and helpless. He tried struggling, but Carson, the ex-sailor, had tied the knots expertly. They didn't give an inch.

He managed to get to his knees, and after a hard struggle, to his feet. He had heard the key turn in the lock after the two men, so he knew there was no use trying to get out that way.

He looked hopefully at the single window, boarded on the outside. If he only had that hatchet now! But it had dropped from his hand when Carson grabbed him out there. And there was no glass in the old cabin's window, or he might have broken it and used a piece to cut his ropes.

It looked as if he might have to stay there until the plotters came back to dispose of him, however they intended to do it. Lugo would have a word to say on that, he knew, and he could expect the worst, whatever that would turn out to be, from Bernardo's cousin.

He listened for sounds outside, his ear pressed to a narrow slit between the boards. He heard nothing at first but the usual small night sounds. Then, all of a sudden, he heard El Capitan Pedro, quite near.

"Juanito! Where are you? Come here at once!" the bird was scolding, in Lugo's voice.

"El Capitan!" Juan called excitedly. "Come!"

And a few moments later, he heard the mynah call from nearby, *"Adelante,* Juanito!" again in Lugo's harshest tones.

He knew it was a very long shot, but he had to try. "Janet, call the police!" he said distinctly, at the slit between the boards, and repeated it over and over. The bird was so quick to pick up words and phrases, perhaps by some miracle he would repeat this where Janet or one of her sisters would hear it!

But the mynah only chattered and whistled and went through a string of useless remarks. And not once did he even try to repeat "Janet, call the police!" for Juan.

So, after awhile, Juan gave it up. It had been only a chance, after all. He thought, with a rueful grin, "If I hadn't wanted him to repeat it, he'd be calling it out all over the woods!"

All he could do now was wait and see what was going to happen to him.

The girls had gone to their own rooms, and lights were out, when they heard Taggart's old jalopy drive away. Dianne guessed that he was taking his friend home.

She paced the floor of her dark bedroom, trying to decide what to do. She wasn't able to put aside a feeling that Janet's arguments against Taggart might make sense. Peggy and Kathy seemed to like and trust the runaway, if that was what he really was. Maybe she was misjudging him. Perhaps it would be a good idea to call the police now and ask them to come out tonight instead of waiting till morning.

But suppose Taggart hadn't told them about the boy as he claimed! And if he hadn't, she could guess what the sergeant would say when she called about it. She would be laughed at and accused of trying to get publicity for the Lennon Sisters, just as she had been when she phoned about hearing the mountain lion that Taggart had said was prowling around!

There was a knock on her door, and her sisters came trooping in, fully dressed, all carrying flashlights.

"Why aren't you all in bed?" she asked sternly.

"Same reason you're not, I guess," Peggy answered soberly. "We've been talking it over, and we still think Juan is the one who's telling the truth, not Mr. Taggart!"

"And we think you should call the police, right now, and tell them all about it!" Janet added firmly. "They can come out and surprise those pirates."

"I've been thinking about it," Dianne admitted, "but I'm afraid that sergeant at police headquarters will answer the phone, and he'll remember I called before, and he'll say, same as he did about the fake lion, that it's only an attempt to get free publicity before the benefit tomorrow night!"

"Can't say I'd blame him much," Peggy admitted.

Janet peeked out the window anxiously, but couldn't see anything of Juan. "He ought to be back by now," she told Kathy anxiously. "I think we should go downstairs and look outside for him."

"We'll do nothing of the sort," Dianne spoke up severely. "I'm still not sure he's telling the truth." She made up her mind suddenly. "I'm going to phone."

"Let's all go," Kathy urged. "It's spooky, waiting here in the dark. And anyhow, you shouldn't be by yourself."

"All right," Dianne smiled, "come along, everybody. One for all and all for one!" She led the way into the hall and along it, flashing her light ahead, to their father's room at the front of the house.

"Let's not switch on the light. I can phone in the dark. There's no use letting anybody outside know we're still up." She crossed the room to the desk where the telephone sat, and picked it up, while the girls stood close around her. She dialed the operator and waited a moment. "Hello?" she said briskly. "Hello, Operator!" But there was no answering voice in her ear. She put her hand over the mouthpiece and told the girls, "The operators must go to bed early in Holiday Town. There's no answer."

Kathy and Janet giggled, but Peggy said, "Yell and jiggle the button. That'll wake her up!"

Dianne called loudly, "Operator! Hello!" and tapped the connection button on the stand. "Nothing," she said. She set the phone back into the cradle, and then picked it up again hopefully and listened. "Phone's dead."

Peggy took it from her and listened. Then she handed it back. "Right, real dead! That's funny! Maybe the storm—"

Kathy shook her head. "I've used it since then. It was okay this morning."

"Let's try the one in the kitchen," Dianne said very quietly, but she was beginning to worry.

They all went down into the kitchen, in the dark, and Dianne tried that phone. It was dead, too.

"Maybe somebody's cut the wires! I saw that in a television show!" Janet said, wide-eyed at the idea.

"It's probably coffee-break time at the central office," Dianne said, trying to be casual. "We'll try again in a few minutes." But she knew there was more than that wrong! There would have been some sort of sound if the phone were in working order.

Janet was probably right. Someone had cut the wires. But there was still the big question. Who had done it? Was it Ben Taggart—or was it young Juan?

And whichever one it was, she and her sisters had been cut off from help!

16   *The Mask Comes Off*

They waited silently for Dianne to pick up the kitchen phone and try to raise the operator at Holiday Town. And when she took down the receiver, listened silently, and then replaced the instrument, Kathy looked at Peggy and nodded, and Peggy said quietly, "The wires are cut, aren't they, Deedee?"

"I'm afraid so," Dianne answered honestly. "There's no use pretending they aren't."

"Ooh!" Janet clenched her fists fiercely. "That horrible old man! Now we know Juan told the truth!"

"Unless Juan cut the wires!" Kathy said. "He could have, you know. To keep us from calling the police."

"I don't believe it!" Janet said firmly. Then she added triumphantly, "He didn't know you intended to call them, but old Creepy Taggart did!"

211

"That's right!" Peggy agreed quickly.

"Hey, wait a minute! I've got an idea!" Janet dashed across the big kitchen to the hardware drawer where the keys were kept. She used her flashlight to look through the drawer, and finally turned around, holding up a long piece of wire. "Let's find where it was cut, and stick this wire in to connect it again!"

Dianne took the wire and examined it quickly. "It isn't the right kind of wire, honey," she said, shaking her head. "You couldn't use it for that."

Kathy and Peggy looked as disappointed as Janet did, but almost at once Peggy exclaimed, "Maybe you couldn't talk over this wire, but I bet you could make noises that would bring some kind of an answer—like 'S O S'! How does that go?"

"I know!" Janet tapped out the letters in Morse code on the nearest flat surface, which happened to be a frying pan. "Three short, three long, three short!"

"That's it! Dot dot dot dash dash dash dot dot dot!" Dianne agreed. "Let's go see what we can find out! If the cut wire is anywhere we can reach, maybe we can get help!"

"Let me go with you!" Janet insisted. But Peggy thought *she* should go, and Kathy wanted to, too. So Dianne settled the matter by saying she would go alone.

"That way, I can hide if I see anybody. It's easier for one."

"But we'll just die, not knowing if you're all right," Janet protested. "Look, I'll bring the big salad scissors to defend us."

"No, no, no!" Dianne refused sternly. "Keep the scissors right here, and a knife or whatever you can put your hands on. And I promise if I run into anything scary, I'll yell blue murder. And you can all come out and save me!" She said it lightly, but there was an undercurrent of fear that she couldn't keep out of her voice.

"Okay," Janet agreed with a sigh. And when Dianne had slipped out of the kitchen, to trace the phone wires back toward the telephone pole, all three of the girls armed themselves with sharp kitchen utensils and waited by the half-open door, tense and nervous.

Dianne didn't have to trace the wire very far. Only a foot or two away from the kitchen door, where the wire was stapled to the wood on its way up to the roof, someone had hacked it apart and it stuck out in the shrubbery, ends dangling uselessly.

Dianne looked at the piece of wire in her hands, and at the dangling wires. "Which one should I try to make the S O S on?" she wondered. She knew one was for incoming sounds and one for outgoing. But which was which? "For once I'm sorry I'm not a boy and haven't had things like this to learn in school!" she thought exasperatedly.

There was only one thing to do and that was to make the S O S first on one dangling wire and then on the other. One was bound to sound in the telephone office, she hoped!

She knelt down and pushed aside the thick-growing shrubbery, but as she was starting to touch the loose wire with the one from the kitchen drawer, the lights of a car came suddenly around from the front driveway and shone full on her.

She jumped to her feet and stood a second in the glare of the headlights, the wire in her hand. The car seemed to rush at her, and she barely had time to jump aside and cower against the house, when it swept past her so closely that it sent a blast of air and dust over her.

She caught a glimpse of two men in the car, and then it started backing rapidly toward her. It was Taggart's old jalopy, and he was at the wheel.

She swung up onto the kitchen step as the car came roaring crazily backwards, zigzagging as it came.

There was a splintering sound as the wheels ripped off

the front of the step, but Dianne had backed into the kitchen a split second before the car got there.

She almost fell into the room. "Quick! Slam the door and bolt it!" she gasped.

Peggy obeyed quickly, and they heard the motor roar and saw the lights flash by the window a second time.

"Who was it?" Kathy asked tremulously.

"Taggart! He tried to run over me!" Dianne was badly shaken. She could hardly speak. "He saw me trying—to fix the wire—and he drove right at me! And when he saw he'd missed me, he backed up and tried again!"

They stood looking at each other in the semidarkness, badly frightened now.

"What are we going to do now?" Kathy whispered, with a shiver. "Do you think he'll try to break in and—" She stopped, but they all knew what she was going to say. If he tried to run over Dianne, he might break in and kill them all! It sounded fantastic, but it could be true.

"He must be out of his mind! Or he's been drinking!" Peggy said, and she went over and made sure she had bolted the door securely.

"I guess now you know Juan was telling the truth about those men!" Janet said soberly. Then she suddenly gave an exclamation, "Gosh, I just remembered! I bet they've caught him! And it's my fault because I told old Taggart that Juan was going to get evidence against them!" She started to cry.

"Janet, dear, please—if they have, it isn't your fault. Don't cry. I don't think Taggart paid any attention to what you said," Dianne assured her. "Do you, girls?"

"Of course not," Peggy said quickly. "Juan is probably being smart, staying away from the house so they will think he's gone. Maybe he's even gone to the police, if he managed to get into the cabin and get one of those guns they were talking about."

But Janet, though she stopped crying, shook her head. "He wouldn't go to the police. They wouldn't believe him, on account of what his cousin has told them about him stealing money." And she refused to be consoled.

There was no sound of the car motor now, but they could hear voices, Taggart's and someone else's, rather loud. The voices seemed to come from Taggart's quarters, and they were accompanied by the clink of glasses, and once, the sound of a bottle being smashed, and then loud guffaws.

Then they heard heavy, uneven steps coming from that direction, and Dianne put aside the curtain on the window a few inches and watched the big, heavy-set man who was coming unsteadily toward the kitchen door. She hadn't seen him before, but knew he must be the one who had come in Taggart's car. He was in pirate costume.

The girls waited tensely, each of them gripping some sort of makeshift weapon, from a kitchen knife to a vinegar cruet. There was a heavy knock on the door.

"Don't let's answer!" Janet whispered. "Make believe we're not here!"

"I'm sure he knows better!" Dianne said quietly. Then she called out, making her voice as calm and unafraid as she could. "Who's there? And what do you want?"

"Wanta talk to you!" The man's voice was as rough as his appearance, though it sounded as if he were trying to be friendly and playful. But his words were slurred. Dianne felt sure he had been drinking heavily. "I'm a friend. Wanta tell you to stay inside the house, an' don't you try an' run away. If you don't do like I say, the bogy man'll get ya, for sure. *I* wouldn't hurt nice li'l girls like you, but somebody else might get sore if you don't do like I say. Understand?" He hiccuped loudly, twice. "Jus' don't go wanderin' around tonight. There's a lot of people goin' to be very busy here before mornin' an' it wouldn't be a good idea if you ran into them. Savvy?"

"Yes, of course. And thank you for telling us. We're going to bed now. Good night!" Dianne called through the door.

" 'S all right, ladies. Just stay there, an' you can come out when the sun's up nice an' warm tomorrow an' we've gone sailin' over the briny foam!" And they heard him stumble away, singing off key, "A life on the ocean wave, ho ho! A home on the rolling deep!"

"Did you hear that? People busy here! That means they're going to take the guns away tonight, I bet!" Janet whispered excitedly. "Gosh! If we could only get to the police and tell them!"

"Maybe we could, somehow! Slip past him and old Taggart, I mean," Kathy suggested.

"And how would we convince the police it wasn't a fancy publicity stunt for the Lennon Sisters?" Peggy asked flatly.

"Juan's bringing a gun or something," Janet started, then she stopped abruptly, remembering. "Only, where is he?" She pushed the window curtain aside and stared out toward the back yard. "If I could get by Taggart and the other one, I bet I know where to find Juan!" And she told them about the chimneylike entrance from the hill down into the cave.

But Dianne refused to let her try to get to the hill alone, past the unknown dangers she might run into if the tipsy man had been telling the truth. "I'm sure if Juan did get some evidence, like a gun, from the cabin, he'd have brought it straight here as he promised. I'm afraid they may have caught him at it."

"Then, we ought to try and get hold of one of those guns ourselves!" Peggy said quickly. "Somehow!"

"Somehow! That's a big word!" Dianne made a grimace.

Janet was peeking out at the side of the curtain again, and she called softly to them, "Hey, look! Taggart and his friend. They're going to the car."

They crowded around Janet, watching. But it was only Taggart who got into the car. And the big man who had come unsteadily out of the house with him stood beside the car, hanging onto it. Taggart seemed to be giving him orders, pointing toward the kitchen.

Janet stealthily opened the window a couple of inches, and they listened intently. They could hear snatches of the conversation at the car.

"But I oughta go lend a hand to Lugo and the boys out at the cabin. Them crates are heavy!" the big man was insisting loudly.

"They've got plenty of help! You'll do better just stayin' here to keep an eye on the house. If the kids try to sneak out, herd 'em back, even if you have to get tough with 'em!" Ben Taggart's voice sounded sharp, and not at all like a kind old caretaker's. "I'll get Lugo to send Parker or one of the boys back to help you cover both the front and rear."

"Aw, why can't I help with the loadin' instead?" the big man objected, and they saw that he tried to open the car door and get in, in spite of Taggart. But Taggart thrust his arm against the big man's chest and pushed him away from the car.

"You're lucky I don't let you!" he snarled. "If Duran saw you the way you are, he'd heave you overboard!"

The big man reached toward his belt and half drew a long-nosed revolver which was remarkably modern looking, compared to his pirate outfit. He had trouble getting it free of the wide silk band, and by the time he had disentangled it clumsily, Taggart had started the car and was driving off across the rear yard.

"Hey! Come back here!" the big man bellowed, waving his gun wildly after Taggart. But Taggart drove on, and after a moment of indecision, the big man thrust his revolver back into his sash and turned away.

They watched from the dark kitchen as he began pacing up and down, weaving a bit.

"He can't watch both doors at the same time!" Janet whispered eagerly. "Why don't we sneak out the front?"

"I'll try it!" Kathy said quickly. "Stay here."

But both Dianne and Peggy protested, and insisted on going with her or being the one to go alone.

It was settled for them, for the time being, by the sound of voices outside. And to their dismay, they saw another burly pirate coming from the direction of the cabin, and heard their guard greet him heartily as "Parker."

"You should have let me go while we had a chance," Janet sulked. "Now what can we do, with two of them watching?"

The two men conferred a minute, and then the newcomer took up a position where he could watch the kitchen door without stirring himself too much. He lit a pipe and settled down, while the big pirate went on up to the front of the house, whistling gaily.

Just before he disappeared from their sight, the girls heard him call back, "Don't let 'em scare you off, Parker. They're real harmless little ladies!" and he laughed heartily.

"I know my job, Carson!" the newcomer called harshly. "Don't worry!"

The girls exchanged worried looks. "Looks like we're sort of pinned down, now," Peggy said glumly.

"Poor Juan!" Kathy said softly, "I wonder what happened to him."

Janet started to sniffle at the mention of Juan, but she stopped suddenly and exclaimed, "I got an idea!"

She bounced away from the window and over to the shelf where they had put the empty tomato can with its rosined string. "Here! Let's try it on them! Maybe they don't know Mr. Taggart's trick!"

"You mean, in here? What good will that do? Even if he heard the most horrible screams, Carson wouldn't try to come in here, and the other one wouldn't either, from the rough way he talks. We could be gobbled up by a dragon and neither of them would give a rap!" Peggy said.

"Peg's right. Neither of them's the hero type!" Kathy agreed.

"But if we staged it so they heard it outside," Dianne was thinking fast, "we could lean out a side window upstairs and—"

"Come on, let's do it! If we keep talking, maybe more of those pirates will be coming here, and then we never will get past them!" Janet urged.

And they moved quickly out of the kitchen to try it.

17 *Dangerous Venture*

Dianne led her sisters quietly to the front hall, and they stopped for a final conference in the dark at the foot of the stairs.

"Janet and I will wait till we hear you yelling out the bedroom window to Carson and the other one, and then we'll slip out and get away to the cabin," she told Kathy and Peggy.

"We think we should do that part of it," Kathy objected. "Why don't you and Janet stay here and make the noises?"

"Because Deedee and I can run faster'n you!" Janet explained hastily. "And you're the ones who made horrible shrieks on that tin can out in the berry patch! You're real experts!" Which bit of flattery won the argument, and Peggy and Kathy started up the stairs to try the trick.

But Dianne was uneasy. "Wait, girls," she said soberly.

"Maybe we'd better not try it. We may be safer if we just stay quiet and don't have anything to say to those men."

But the others disagreed. "I think we owe it to Juan to try to stop those gun smugglers, now that we realize he was telling the truth about them to Janet," Peggy said.

"And we'd better hop to it, because it's getting along toward morning," Kathy reminded them, "and Carson said we'd be allowed to come outside when the sun was up. That must mean they plan to be gone by that time."

"Let's hurry, then, and don't forget to put on a good act up there, kids!" Dianne kept her voice light.

"Don't worry! Sarah Bernhardt has nothing on the Lennons!" Peggy couldn't resist a giggle.

Then Kathy and she hurried upstairs with the old tomato can and its rosined string, and let themselves into one of the rooms on the side of the house away from the kitchen. They had a little trouble opening the window without making any noise. They saw Carson below as he walked past, whistling and still lurching a little tipsily. Then when he was out of sight around the corner of the house in the direction of the front door, they began prying up the window an inch at a time, and finally had it open enough for Peggy to lean out with the tin can. She held the contraption out of the window and gave a series of jerks on the string, some short and some long.

The sounds she got out of the tin can were even more weird and scary than the ones old Taggart had managed to get from it. They ranged from low moans and growls to wild shrieks, and all in the space of less than half a minute.

And when the last wailing scream had died away, Peggy ducked back into the room, and they closed the window quickly and silently.

They peered down from behind the curtain, and for a moment, no one came in sight. Then, Carson's head was poked around the corner of the house, very cautiously, as he studied the moonlit grounds. Seeing nothing to account for the noises, he eased himself around all the way, and stood with drawn revolver, glaring around threateningly.

"Now!" Peggy whispered, and then flung open the window with a bang, and leaned out to call down loudly, "What was that horrible noise? Did you hear it?"

"Sure did!" He blinked up at her. "Sounded like it came from right around here!" He looked uneasily toward the dark bulk of the oak thicket a dozen yards away, and took a tighter grip on his gun.

Peggy gave a good imitation of a shriek of dismay, which was Kathy's cue to push her head out past Peggy and call down excitedly, "Please look around and see if you can find out what it was! We've heard it before, and Mr. Taggart said it was a ghost! It must be in there!" She pointed excitedly toward the thicket.

Carson stared uneasily where she indicated, but he made no attempt to go investigate. And at that moment Parker strode up, his own gun drawn. He cast a brief look at the girls up at the window, and then demanded roughly, "What was that yelling about? What's going on here?"

"That's what we're trying to find out!" Peggy called down to him. "We think it's something in there!" She pointed to the thicket again. "Something screeching!"

Parker gave Carson a rough push. "Snap out of it, Brick. What was the racket?"

"I dunno," Carson admitted uneasily, still staring at the dark wilderness of underbrush. "Sounded like wildcats!"

"Yeah, or mountain lions! That's how it sounded to me from where I was!" He took a couple of steps toward the brush, then saw that Carson wasn't following him. "Come on, let's look around a bit!"

"Not me!" Carson even backed up a couple of steps as

he spoke loudly. "Let 'em settle their own fights! I don't crave to get all clawed up! Go by yourself if you're that nosy!"

Parker wasn't. He came back, rather relieved, it seemed to the girls. "Okay, girls!" He called up to them. "Take it easy now. Go on back to sleep, all of you! You ain't in any danger."

Kathy called out, in a scared voice, "Please don't go too far away, in case they come back here!"

It was Carson who answered her. "We'll be right close, miss. But you better close that window, now. Cats can sure climb fast!"

He was amused to see the girls disappear at once, and the window get slammed shut. He turned to Parker with a hearty laugh, "Told you they were a scary bunch. No chance of them tryin' to run out. They won't put their noses outside the rest of the night!"

"Just the same," Parker said sharply, "we'll keep on watchin' both doors!" And he went briskly out of sight around the corner of the house to resume his vigil outside the kitchen door.

But he was a couple of minutes late. Dianne and Janet were already out and gone, running lightly now across the dark rear yard toward the back gate.

The gate hinges were squeaky, and they didn't dare risk opening it for fear Parker would hear. So they went over it without much trouble, except that Janet snagged her slacks on a nail and it seemed for a horrible moment that she might have to leave part of them behind her. But Dianne helped her down, and they hurried on around the base of the hill and through the chaparral and cactus toward the old log cabin in the box canyon.

The moment they came in sight of the cabin, they saw that they were going to have quite a job getting the evidence of smuggling that they had come for. The front door was standing open, and there was a glow of lantern light streaming out. Shadows moved across the open door, and the girls could hear the indistinct murmur of men's voices from inside.

Then, abruptly, the light from the doorway was blocked off by the bulky figures of two men in pirate costume carrying out a packing box between them. It wasn't a large box, but it seemed very heavy, by the way the men were grunting and straining as they started up over the hill behind the cabin with it.

"Where are they going up there?" Dianne whispered.

"The yacht's in a big cove on the other side of the next hill. That's where the cattle nearly ran over Peg and me when we were trying to find a trail down to the beach to watch the 'movie actors' perform!" Janet gave a little snicker. "Wouldn't it be funny if they bumped into some of those cattle?"

Dianne shuddered. "I hope they don't! No matter who those men are, it wouldn't be at all funny!"

Janet snorted softly. "Unless it was old Taggart! I still think he started that stampede."

"Speaking of the devil," Dianne said quietly, "look."

This time the oblong of light that was the open doorway of the cabin revealed Ben Taggart carrying a small wooden box on his shoulder. It wasn't over two feet square, but it weighed him down.

They saw him stop in the doorway and look back into the room. Even at that distance, they could see his black scowl. Then he came out and closed the door behind him, and in the moonlight they saw him start up the hill along the path the other two men had taken.

"Looks like he's the last!" Janet whispered.

"We can't take a chance. We're not going in till we're sure he *is* the last. And the only way to know, is to look inside!" Dianne puzzled over it.

"If there's a window—" Janet began. Then she grabbed Dianne's arm. "Come on. I see one. Let's go."

They moved quickly toward the side window, but when they ventured close, they saw that it was boarded, and wouldn't be a way either in or out. There was a narrow space between the heavy boards, and the lamplight was shining out.

"At least we can look inside and see if there's anything left that we can pick up to show the police!" Janet whispered. "You watch and listen for footsteps on the hill, and I'll peek in."

So Dianne stayed back in the shadow, every nerve on edge with suspense, listening for a sound that would mean some of the men were coming back. And Janet crept quickly up to the boarded window and peered in.

To her amazement, she saw Juan, his hands and feet tied securely, sitting only a few feet away from the window, on the dirt floor.

Her first impulse was to speak to him at once, but she stopped herself. There might be someone else there, guarding him. Then she had an idea. There was a certain little noise that Juan's friend El Capitan Pedro made in his throat, a little purring sound. She would see what Juan would do if he heard it.

It took a couple of tries before she got the sound just like the one the mynah bird had made, but when she did get it exactly right, she was delighted to see Juan's eager look toward the crack between the boards.

"Capitan!" Juan said guardedly, but loudly enough to prove to his listener that he must be alone. "Listen to me! Say, 'Janet, call the police, Janet, call the police.'"

"Juan! It's me! I'm here!" Janet put her lips close to the narrow crack. "Deedee and I are right outside!"

"You must go away quickly before the men return for more guns! You are in great danger!" Juan told her rapidly, struggling helplessly with the ropes around his hands. "You cannot help me except by bringing the police!"

"How soon will the men be back?" Janet persisted.

"A few minutes! Go, please!"

But Janet had run away from the window, and was already opening the door. There she turned and vigorously waved to Dianne to come quickly.

Dianne ran to the cabin as fast as she could. Janet was trying her best to untie the rope from Juan's hands, but she wasn't having any success with the tight knots.

"Let it go! Hurry away, both of you! I will be all right. They are taking me aboard the yacht after everything else is loaded. At least, I think so!" Juan was honest.

"If they don't drop you in the ocean on the way!" Janet was just as honest.

"If we only had a knife!" Dianne tried to help with the ropes.

"There is the hatchet I took from your garage!" Juan said eagerly. "It should be on the ground outside the window. It cuts well!"

Janet was out of the cabin like a flash, and back again a half minute later, with the hatchet.

With Dianne's help, she cut the rope on Juan's hands, and the moment they were free, Juan chopped the ropes that bound his feet.

Then the two girls helped him to his feet, and though it was agony to walk, after his ankles had been tightly bound so long, Juan managed to hobble to the door, between them.

"Hold it a minute!" Janet stopped abruptly. "We want something to show the police in Holiday Town that we haven't made up the story."

Juan pointed. "Over there in the corner, in that crate

which has been opened. You will find machine-gun cartridges. Bring a box of the ones in the red-marked cartons. They are the ball cartridges for the submachine guns which it is against the law to own. But hurry!"

Janet darted across the room and dug a box of ammunition out of the crate. It was quite heavy, but she gamely put it on her shoulder and rejoined the others at the door. "Sure hope this will convince them," she said. "I'd hate to lug it for miles for nothing!"

Then the three hurried out, closing the door after them. In the darkness, they started to make their way back toward the house.

Dianne stopped suddenly. "Over there in that shed, isn't that Taggart's jalopy? Why don't we take it and make a run past the house in it?"

"Oh, Deedee! That's a wonderful idea!" Janet exclaimed.

They hurried toward the old shed, Janet and the cartridge box bringing up the rear. Dianne touched the hood as she went toward the driver's seat. "It's still a little warm. It should start easily."

She got up into the seat, and felt around in the dark for the ignition key. Ben Taggart had said a couple of times that he always left the key there, because if he took it with him he would be sure to drop it some place around the ranch and be stuck without a car till he found it again. He had had it happen once or twice in the past.

Juan and Janet got in quickly beside her. "Let's get moving!" Janet urged. "Step on it, gal!"

But Dianne turned a white face to them. "There isn't any key here. For once he took it with him!"

"Wouldn't you know it!" Janet said disgustedly. "Okay. We get out and walk!" And she hopped out, followed by Juan, who was carrying the box of cartridges now. Dianne followed them after one hopeful look around the floor of the car to be sure the key hadn't merely dropped out of the lock.

They started out of the shed to cross the clearing between them and the narrow road at the foot of the hill. Juan stopped them abruptly and drew them back into the shadow of the shed. "Look!" He pointed up toward the top of the hill.

The tall figure of old Ben Taggart was silhouetted against the sky as he came over the hill and started down toward the cabin.

"We'd better run for it!" Janet whispered.

But even as she was saying it, Janet knew that it was too

late. The moonlight was too bright in the clearing. The moment they tried to get over to the road, Taggart couldn't help seeing them.

And after Taggart had already tried to run over Dianne, they knew they couldn't hope that he would let them go.

They were trapped.

18 *Escape*

It was too late to try to cross the moonlit clearing without Taggart seeing them from high on the hill behind the cabin. They must stay where they were until he had gone into the cabin, and then make a break for the thick chaparral where they possibly could hide.

Another man was following Taggart over the hill, and they were talking back and forth as they came. Their voices came clearly through the still night air.

"When do we pick up the kid and take him to the ship?" the second man asked.

"Duran says leave him till all the crates are aboard. He figures Lugo will be here by then, and can give the kid a talkin' to before we take him," Taggart called back as they wound their way down the hillside.

"Talkin' with his fists, you mean!" the other man

laughed. "I know Lugo!"

In the shadows of the shed, Janet reached out and patted Juan's hand. "We'll fool 'em!" she whispered, managing a little grin that she meant to be reassuring. "They've got to get hold of you first! Let's make a run for it the minute they go inside the house!"

"No," Juan shook his head slowly, "I think it would be better if I go back now and give myself up. I am sure my cousin will not be angry, if I pretend that I was just joking when I told you I would make trouble."

"You know he won't believe that!" Dianne whispered.

"I think he might. And you and Janet can hurry away at once and go to the police and the coast guard with your evidence. They will stop the yacht and find the guns." Juan was trying to be very convincing and firm.

But neither girl believed that he felt as sure of his own safety as he pretended.

"Go, the moment they enter the house! I will follow them inside and—"

"And you won't fool them for a minute!" Janet added quickly. "And you're not fooling us, either! You *know* old Taggart might even take a shot at you!"

"But it is the only—" Juan started, but Dianne interrupted.

"Giving yourself up won't do us any good, Juan," Dianne said quietly. "The minute they see those cut ropes in there, they'll know somebody helped you get away. And they'll hunt for us just as much as if you stay right with us and we try to get away together."

The two men had reached the foot of the hill alongside the cabin, and were entering. A moment later there was a yell of surprise and rage, and old Taggart came charging out again, flourishing his shotgun.

The other man followed him. "What are you getting so excited about? Maybe Lugo came along and cut him loose! He might be takin' him to the ship by a different trail than the one we've been using!"

"Yeah," old Taggart pulled at his walrus mustache. "Yeah, maybe so. There ain't anybody else could cut him loose. We got them Lennon kids shut up tight in the house."

"Well, that proves it was Lugo," the other man said. "Let's load up an' get a couple more crates over the hill."

"Okay," Taggart agreed, and they started back into the cabin. "Only, I don't know what trail Lugo an' the kid could've took, without us seein' them."

"Aw, quit worryin'," the other man laughed. "Lugo

knows his way around this island. He's lived here longer than you."

They went on into the cabin, and Janet gave an explosive sigh of relief. "Oh, boy! What a break!" She laughed.

"We're lucky!" Dianne smiled. "Now let's get started before Mr. Taggart has any more doubts and starts hunting around here for Juan!"

"Wait a sec!" Janet ran to the jalopy, fiddled with the air valve on one of the front tires, and stood grinning with satisfaction as the air whooshed out of the tire and the jalopy settled crazily on three wheels. "That might slow him down if he does!"

They hurried across the moonlit clearing, keeping a weather eye on the open front door of the cabin, beyond which the two men were talking casually now.

"How can we get by the guards at the house, Carson and the other fellow?" Janet asked Dianne in a whisper, as they moved into the thick underbrush at the foot of the hill and started along the path toward the ranch yard.

"We'll hope Carson is sleeping off his celebration," Dianne told her, "or at any rate, too sleepy to be very watchful!"

They went on a few steps, and then, suddenly Juan held

out his hand to stop them. "I hear something. It sounds like a car!"

They heard it, too, then. It was coming from the direction of the ranch house. A moment afterward, they saw the headlights silhouette the shoulder of the hill that lay ahead of them.

They barely had time to duck off the narrow road and drop flat behind clumps of cactus beside it, when Lugo's panel truck came into sight around the corner and passed within a few feet of them. Lugo was at the wheel, and they didn't see anyone else with him.

"Hurry! Hurry!" Juan urged the girls, and all three began to move fast along the road.

But Janet, turning her head to look back at the cabin, stumbled over a rock and fell headlong. Dianne heard her fall, stopped at once, and came back to help her up. Juan ran back, too, casting anxious looks toward the cabin, where Taggart and the other man had run out to meet Lugo's car.

"I'm okay. Come on!" Janet was unhurt, just shaken a little by her fall.

An excited conference was going on at the side of Lugo's car now, and it sounded as if Lugo were blaming Taggart for not guarding the boy better. Taggart in turn was angrily defending himself.

Dianne helped Janet hobble along the road, and Juan brought up the rear. He glanced back from time to time, and suddenly gave an exclamation of alarm. "He is coming this way, and Taggart is circling past the shed! The other man has gone part way up the hill to look there for us!" He groaned. "They will soon have us trapped!"

The girls stared back, and saw that Juan was right. Lugo was striding along, a mean-looking revolver dangling from his right hand. And Taggart's shotgun reflected moonlight, as he held it in readiness to use on the fugitive.

"You should have let me give myself up!" Juan told Dianne in a whisper. "But it is still not too late!"

He started to get up, and was still on his knees when they heard a voice from somewhere near the cabin. It said, sounding exactly like Juan himself, "Lugo! Lugo!"

Juan gasped. "It is El Capitan!" he told the girls.

Lugo had left the narrow path now, and was hurrying toward the clump of brush from which the voice had come.

"So there you are, you stupid brat!" he shouted. "I will settle with you!" And he took wild cuts at the shrubbery with his clubbed gun as he went deeper into the tangle.

"Lugo! Lugo!" Juan's voice said, this time from ten more feet in front of Lugo.

"Don't try to get away! I'll teach you to spy on me!" Lugo was raving.

"Quick! There's nobody near the car now!" Janet pointed. "Let's grab it!"

All three scrambled to their feet then, and made a rush through the cactus and scrub oak toward the car.

They had almost reached it, when the man on the hill yelled, "Lugo! The car!" and took a wild shot toward the running trio.

Lugo was too intent on trying to catch the boy he thought was slipping away from him in the shrubbery. He paid no attention to the man's warning cry.

And then the two girls and Juan were at the car, into the driver's seat, and Dianne had started up the motor with a loud roar.

Taggart came running from the shed, waving his shotgun and yelling, "Stop or I'll shoot!"

But Dianne gunned the motor and the car leaped forward, turned, and headed back toward the ranch. A shot from Taggart's gun missed by a wide margin as it sped away. And Chris Lugo, running now to head off the fugitives, barred their way suddenly in the road, his revolver menacing them.

"Get down!" Dianne told the others, and put her foot down hard on the accelerator. They passed only a couple of feet wide of Chris Lugo, who jumped back, tripped and went sprawling. His revolver discharged harmlessly into the air as he fell, and by the time he had scrambled to his feet again, the racing panel truck was out of sight around the foot of the hill.

Taggart ran up to him. "My car's right there. We better get after him!"

They ran, joined by the third man, to the shed. But thanks to Janet's foresight, there was one very flat tire on the old bag of bolts.

"We got to stop them!" Taggart shouted, "Come on!"

And all three started to run after the car. But after running a few yards, Lugo stopped suddenly. "Wait!" he called to the others. And when they stopped to hear what he had to say, Lugo explained. "The boys at the house must have heard the shots. They'll stop him!"

"Just the same," Taggart worried, "we oughta get the rest of the stuff aboard and pull out, in case Carson an' Parker miss."

But Lugo only laughed. "Juan and whoever his friend was won't get far! There's only about half a gallon of gas in the truck! I let it go down because I figured on leavin' it behind when we sail! They won't get halfway to town!"

At the house, the rear gate was open. Lugo hadn't bothered to close it as he went through to the cabin.

Dianne drove the speeding panel truck through the open gate and across the back yard.

Parker heard it coming and got up, yawning, to meet it. "Guess Lugo's come back for us already," he told himself, and glanced at the paling night sky. "They got through loadin' the stuff earlier than they figured."

But when the panel truck careened around the corner of the house, it didn't slow up. It went past so fast that the startled guard hardly had time to recognize that the driver was Dianne Lennon and not Chris Lugo, and that there were others on the driver's seat with her.

"Stop 'em!" he yelled, and fired wildly at the speeding truck's tires, missing by a wide margin.

Brick Carson had been half asleep on the front steps of the big house. The shot and Parker's yell brought him to his feet, dazed and confused. He hadn't yet come to completely when the truck came past at full speed and headed wildly across the lawn toward the road.

Parker ran around the corner of the house yelling, "Stop them! It's the kid and a couple of the Lennon girls! They've swiped the truck!" Parker took aim and shot, but missed again and only succeeded in making Dianne press down the gas lever to the floor as she swung the truck out into the road and headed for town. "Why didn't you shoot?" he barked at Carson.

"Because it ain't possible you saw the kid an' the Lennon girls in that truck! You're always goin' off half-cocked!" he told Parker sleepily. "The kid's tied up in the cabin, an' the girls are in the house!"

And as if to prove he was right, a light went on upstairs just then. "See?" Carson told Parker. "You woke 'em up!"

"I know what I saw!" Parker growled angrily, "and if you'd stayed awake like you oughta, you'd aseen it wasn't Lugo at the wheel!"

And a few minutes later, as Lugo strode up, Carson got another tongue-lashing for his carelessness.

And since it was now almost daylight, all three of them hurried back afoot to join Taggart and the other man carrying the last of the crates of illegal guns and stolen ammunition to the yacht.

It was not till they had moved all but the last crate that Chris Lugo discovered that one of its boxes of machine-gun bullets was missing. Since the box, with its government labeling, would prove that government stores had been looted, Lugo and the others knew that the coast guard would be alerted to search the yacht, once Juan told his story and showed the cartridge box.

The illegal gun parts and their ammunition were being stored among crates of pirate costumes, fake cannon, broadswords, and all the odds and ends of props used to make a pirate movie. There were false bottoms in all the prop crates, and as the men brought aboard the crates of gun parts, the others waiting aboard the yacht hastily stowed them away. All were wearing their costumes, and cameras were conspicuous on deck, with light reflectors and spotlights.

Once the yacht was under way, they would keep a close watch for a coast guard cutter, and at first sight of it, they would go through all the motions of acting and picture filming.

Lugo felt sure they could fool the law. Duran was a smooth talker and knew all the movie lingo. They also had legitimate papers for a filming cruise to Mexico's west coast.

"Do not worry now," he told the others. "We have plenty of time. Even now, the truck has run out of gas. And Juan and those interfering girls cannot be more than halfway to Holiday Town along the private road. They will have to walk five miles to the nearest house. That will take some time!"

But he wasn't exactly right with his prediction. They were almost eight miles along on the private road to the town before the motor began coughing and sputtering and finally stopped altogether.

Dianne sat gripping the wheel and pressing down hard on the gas pedal. But it was no use. "Well, here we are!" she said, with a shrug. "Now we walk!"

Janet sighed. "And by the time we get to town, the yacht will be away out at sea!"

"The coast guard will catch it!" Juan said hopefully.

But Dianne, climbing down into the dusty road, said glumly, "*If* they don't think we're making it all up for publicity, like the police did about the mountain lion!"

"They'd better not act so dumb!" Janet said vehemently. "And I'll tell them so!"

"That should help us a lot!" Dianne couldn't help smiling at Janet's fierceness. She knew that her little sister wasn't

half as bold as she pretended to be, and she would probably
be as meek as a lamb. "But I don't believe it will be necessary
to scold them. Daddy and the family will be here today,
and after we tell him what has been going on, I'm sure he'll
see to it that they admit it isn't a publicity stunt we've been
trying to put over!"

"That's right!" Janet felt better already. "He'll straighten
them out! Let's get walking, before I fall asleep right here,
I'm so tired."

"Maybe we should leave you behind a tree till we get
back!" Dianne laughed, and as they started out, she linked
her arm through Janet's and let the sleepy girl lean on her
as they walked.

Juan silently brought up the rear, glancing behind him
constantly, worried that at any minute they might hear
the sound of pursuit and have to hide.

And, with only another mile to go, he heard the racket of
an old car, coming fast along the road behind them.

"Quick! Off the road! A car is coming!" he warned
them.

And Dianne hastily led sleepy Janet toward the trees that
lined the road. But Janet was far too sleepy to move fast,
and she held back, stumbling along and protesting that she

was tired and just couldn't hurry.

Juan took her other arm, and together, he and Dianne had her almost safe in the shadows under the trees, when the old car careened to a stop only a dozen yards away.

19 *Safe Harbor*

As the car overtook them and came to a quick stop in the middle of the dusty road, Juan jumped to put himself between it and the girls. He hadn't time even to pick up a rock to use in defending them, but he made up his mind to fight as long as he could and give them a chance to run into the woods.

Then, as all three got a good look at the car, they saw to their immense relief that it wasn't Ben Taggart's jalopy as they had feared. It was an ancient rattletrap of even earlier vintage, but painted bravely in vivid red and yellow.

And the girls recognized the smiling and somewhat puzzled face of the young copilot of the airline, Jim West. "What on earth are *you* doing here, Miss Lennon?" he asked Dianne, and before she could answer, he swung out of the little old car and hurried to the girls as they stood staring at him almost as if they didn't believe what they saw.

"Has your car broken down?" he asked, looking around for it and not seeing anything that even looked like a car.

"We ran out of gas back a couple of miles," Janet had found her tongue. "We'd sure like a lift."

"Of course!" Jim West grinned. And then he sobered at once as he looked at Juan and seemed puzzled. "Is the young man with you?"

"Oh, yes! This is Juan Lopez, our very good friend," Janet said hastily. "He's going with us."

And as Jim West still looked puzzled, Dianne said quietly, "We'll explain as we go, if you don't mind giving us a ride into town."

"Delighted! If you'll do me the honor!" He bowed, half in fun, and opened the back door of the car, waving Janet and Juan in. And when they were in, he closed the door, and opened the front one for Dianne to get in beside him. Then he ran around the front of the car and climbed into the driver's seat, grinning back at Juan and Janet. "Just knock those rocks off the seat, kids. I'm a 'rock hound,' you know. I collect specimens on my day off. I was just heading back to make the ten o'clock flight to the mainland.

Hope you don't mind if I hit it up a little!"

"No, indeed!" Janet and Dianne chorused. "Faster the better!"

"Here we go!" And a moment later, with a mighty roar, the car was on its springless way at breakneck speed.

"What got you up so early?" Jim West called to Dianne, over the racket, as he tooled the bucket along straight stretches and around corners on two ancient wheels.

So Dianne, with shouted help from Janet in the back seat, told him the whole story. But Juan was silent, studying the young pilot's face. And he could see that Jim West was not completely convinced that Dianne's story was anything but a bit of fiction.

"He does not believe it," he told Janet quietly.

So Janet tore open the carton of machine-gun shells, took out a handful, and leaned over Jim West's shoulder, holding the cartridges in front of his face. "Look! They had scads of these! And guns that use them! Believe us or not!"

Jim took his eyes off the road long enough to look at the handful of cartridges. He knew what they were. He had used hundreds of them in Korea. "Okay!" he said quickly.

And when he came to the last stretch of road, past the

outlying houses, he turned the car away from town and out toward the coast guard station at the end of the island.

"Hey! Where are you taking us?" Janet demanded.

"Straight to the top!" Jim West called back to her. And a few minutes later, he turned into the coast guard station and pulled up outside of headquarters, leaning on his horn.

For a few minutes, while the sentry argued against disturbing the commanding officer, it seemed that they weren't going to get a chance to tell their story. But a smile from Dianne had more effect than Jim West's argument, and they soon found themselves in the office of the sleepy C. O.

They told the situation in as brief a time as they could, Juan supplying all the details he had overheard about the fake pirates' plans.

"Seems strange they would talk that much in front of you," the gray haired officer said skeptically.

"They were taking me with them, sir. I do not think they planned that I would live very long," Juan said honestly.

The commanding officer reached for his desk phone. "Give me the officer of the day," he ordered crisply. And a moment later, the girls and Juan were delighted to hear him issue orders to intercept the yacht *Starlight* now believed proceeding from Big Cove on the windward side of the island to points south. "Intercept and board. Make search for contraband rifles and machine guns. Usual procedure. Report."

Then he sat back with a sigh. "I hope I'm not sticking out my neck, girls, by buying your story. I must warn you again, before the orders are carried out, that if this is just a made-up story for publicity purposes, someone is going to be very sorry."

"It's all true, sir," Dianne assured him with dignity.

"We know better than to tell fibs to the Government," Janet added. "Daddy says, 'Never fool with Uncle Whiskers!' Doesn't he, Deedee?"

Dianne looked shocked, but the commanding officer laughed heartily. "Your friends on the *Starlight* are going to wish they'd had your daddy's advice!" he told Janet.

Within a few minutes, a sleek coast guard cutter left its berth and proceeded swiftly around the end of the island. A very efficient-looking gun was ready for action on deck.

Jim West stood with the girls and Juan and watched the smart-looking craft disappear. "There they go!" he said. "And if I don't get to Holiday Town in the next few minutes, flight number six is going to be minus one copilot!

Where would you folks like to be dropped?"

Dianne and Janet exchanged looks. They were both thinking of the same thing. The girls would be worried sick about them, out there at the ranch. But they had no way of getting back there to tell them that everything was working out all right now.

"I guess we'd better go to Holiday Town with you," Dianne told Jim West. "Maybe the phone people can send a crew out to fix our phone this morning, and they'll let us ride along."

But when Jim West dropped them off at the office of the local phone company and went on his way, they found that the only emergency crew was at the other end of the island and wouldn't be back for hours.

"I guess we start hiking, then," Janet said gloomily.

But just as she finished speaking, Juan gave an exclamation and pointed up the street. Ben Taggart's old jalopy was coming, swaying and bumping along with one tire so flat that its wheel was riding on the rim. And Peggy was driving, hanging on grimly to the wheel, while Kathy, at her side, desperately tried to keep from being bumped out of the car.

Peggy brought the old wreck to a sudden stop as Janet

ran up, waving and shouting. And Kathy almost went out head over heels.

But a moment later, the girls were all hugging each other and talking excitedly at once, while Juan stood to one side, smiling shy approval.

Before they knew it, a small crowd had gathered. And everyone wanted to know what the excitement was all about.

Janet obligingly told a polite young man a brief outline of their experience, and was startled to see him take off to the nearest phone booth. He was a reporter!

And that was how the news came to Bill Lennon and the rest of the family as they came happily across the channel on the big steamer.

The captain called down the bulletin to his first mate, the first mate relayed it excitedly to several of the crew, and the bewildered Lennon family found themselves surrounded and informed that their girls had taken part in the unmasking and capture of a gang of gunrunners.

And when the steamer drew up at its wharf on the crescent bay of Holiday Town, there was a good-sized crowd of young fans milling around the four Lennon sisters and young Juan.

Juan had tried to slip away several times, but Janet had hung onto his arm and reminded him urgently, "Daddy will want to say thank you for fishing me out of the ocean. Please wait!" and Juan had had to give in.

Only the sight of the neat gray cutter herding the big white yacht past the end of the pier lured the teenage fans away from the Lennon girls to rush out and cheer for the triumphant coast guard. They got an added thrill at the sight of some sheepish-looking prisoners in pirate garb herded on the slightly battered deck of the expensive big yacht.

"Let's go out to the ranch while we can," Mrs. Lennon suggested hurriedly. And they made their way hastily to the big station wagon that Frank Lane had brought to meet them. They were gone by the time the fans gave up cheering the coast guard and came back to look for the Lennons.

Frank Lane beamed happily, as he drove and listened to Janet telling the family all the wild happenings of the week in a confused but happy jumble of times and places.

"I've already spoken to David Gardner in New York, about the excitement on the ranch," he told Bill Lennon, under the clamor of the younger Lennons all demanding more details from Janet. "He's 'jetting' out this afternoon, and he'll be at the benefit tonight."

Juan was lost somewhere under an avalanche of happy, restless youngsters, who were climbing all over him as if he were part of the family. And he liked it. He hadn't realized how lonely a life he had had till he had found himself one of this happy group—one of them now, but still an outsider who would soon be going on his way alone again!

In the front seat, between her father and Frank Lane, Dianne quietly told them all she knew about Juan, and how he had saved Janet's life.

For a while, as they went along the bumpy private road, Bill Lennon was thoughtfully silent. Then he told Dianne, "The boy's had a hard time of it. We must find some way to do something for him."

"I don't think he's had a chance to go to school very much," Dianne told him, softly so that Juan couldn't hear from the back seat. The kids were still raising a happy rumpus back there, but she was careful anyhow, to spare Juan's feelings.

"Then we'll send him, if he wants to go. And on to college, too, if he'll let us."

"Won't you have to get his father's okay? I understand

he's been down in Mexico for several months," Dianne said doubtfully.

"That shouldn't cause too much trouble," Frank Lane broke in. "I've heard he was a good father, very much attached to the boy. I'm sure a letter would bring his hearty acceptance."

But when they arrived at the ranch house, and Bill Lennon had a chance to get acquainted with the boy, he was disappointed to learn that Juan had no idea of how to reach his father in Mexico.

"He may have written to me," Juan admitted, "but if he did, Lugo probably opened the letter for what money it might contain and said nothing about it to me."

"Well, if I can find where he is, you'd like to go to school and maybe college later on, wouldn't you?"

"Oh, *si, si!* Yes, sir!" Juan's eyes sparkled. "It has been the dream of my life to be a man of education! To wear shoes all the time!"

"We'll get after it right away!" Bill Lennon promised. "And now, come along while I get my lazy girls ready to sing at the benefit tonight. I have a hunch they haven't spent much time rehearsing their numbers!"

There was to be an early afternoon birthday party for

Billy before time to leave for the rehearsal before the benefit performance. Each of the Lennon children had a birthday in a different month, and that made ten months in which a party was certain to happen, winter or summer!

Everyone helped get the house ready, and Nana as usual, took on the grandmotherly task of seeing that the cake was baked, iced, and decorated with the proper name, while all but the honored birthday child held giggling secret conferences over the wrapping of surprise gifts.

They pulled Juan into the celebration, and he was soon high on a stepladder hanging festoons of pink and blue and white tissue-paper garlands over the big dining room table where the cake would duly appear for the ceremony of blowing out the candles.

Dianne, Kathy, Peggy and Janet went through the numbers they intended to use that night, and their father was pleasantly surprised. "For once, no clinkers!" he teased them playfully. "But go over your parts a few times more, to make sure."

And while they were cheerfully obeying, Bill Lennon rode back to Holiday Town in the station wagon with Frank Lane.

"I like to get things settled," he told Lane. "I want to

get that letter off to Bernardo Lopez as soon as I can find somebody who knows his address in Mexico."

"Wish I could help—" Frank Lane began. Then he broke off, snapping his fingers, and almost running the big car into the ditch. "I know who'd be sure to know where Lopez is! Padre Antonio of the fishermen's church, near the wharf. They've always been close friends, and the padre will be glad to tell you."

"Good! I'll see him right away!"

"Let me off at my office, if you don't mind. And keep the car to bring the family in to the benefit tonight." He bustled out at the next stop. "See you later, with Mr. Gardner."

"Much obliged," Bill Lennon called after him, and turned the car toward the modest little church near the fishing pier.

Padre Antonio was tall and spare, with deep-set dark eyes and skin bronzed by years of service to the men of the water front. There was still a faint trace of accent in his quiet voice, as he welcomed his visitor.

When he had heard what Bill Lennon wished to do for young Juan Lopez for saving Janet's life, the parish priest of the fishermen sat silent a long time. "Yes," he said at last, "I know where Bernardo is. Only today, strange as it seems, I had a letter from him."

"Good!" Bill Lennon took out his pen and a piece of paper. "Do you mind letting me have his address? I'll need his okay to send Juan to a good mainland school."

"It will not be necessary," the Padre said. "I think you will understand when you read this letter."

20 *The Answer*

Bill Lennon put down the letter that Padre Antonio had given him to read. "Well!" he said, "that *is* a surprise. It clears the way for me to send Juan to school, of course, but it's going to be a sad blow to the boy!"

"Perhaps not," the kindly old priest told him, "now that he has made new friends, your girls and yourself. He always seemed a lonely little fellow, in spite of Bernardo's affection for him. Now we understand!"

"But to find out suddenly, in a few written words, that he isn't really Bernardo's son, that he's really alone in the world!" Lennon frowned. "At least, Bernardo Lopez could have written directly to the boy to say that he wasn't coming back to this country and explained why he never told him they were not really related."

"Perhaps he thought it could make no difference to

either of them," Padre Antonio sighed.

Bill Lennon tapped the letter with his finger, and smiled, with a shake of his head, "Then he marries a widow with six children and everything changes!"

"His duty is to them," Padre Antonio smiled and gave a slight Latin shrug of his shoulders. "That's life."

"I suppose we'd better let Juan know. I hate to think of it, poor kid!"

"Let him be happy tonight," Padre Antonio suggested. "Tomorrow is time enough to tell him."

"Would you do it, Padre? Maybe after Mass you could drop out for noonday dinner with us, and break the news to him afterwards."

"Perhaps that would be best," the gray-haired priest agreed. And then his eyes twinkled. "And the good dinner will be welcome, after my own poor cooking!"

"We have the best chefs in the world!" Bill Lennon assured him cheerfully as they shook hands. "I'll warn them they've been challenged!"

And when Bill Lennon got back to the ranch house half an hour later, he found the birthday party in full swing and everyone having the usual good time—including Juan, whose happiness shone on his face as the kids counted him in on all their games. Padre Antonio's decision to put off telling Juan about the letter had been a happy one.

Now the birthday cake—combined effort of Nana, Mom Lennon, and Expert Decorator Dianne—was brought to the table, and Billy was urged to make a wish and blow out the candles.

"Come on, Birthday Child! The candles are burning down!" Janet laughed.

But Billy shook his head shyly. "Juan says he doesn't know when his birthday is, so I want to give him mine for today. Here, Juan, you blow out the candles and wish!"

Juan held back uncertainly, but the clamor of agreement from all the Lennons finally persuaded him, and he gave a great puff that blew out every candle at once.

"Hooray! He gets his wish!" Pat and Danny chorused. Then they all marched around Juan and Billy and sang "Happy Birthday!" loudly and happily.

Bill let the celebration go on awhile longer, but he called Mrs. Lennon aside and talked seriously to her about Juan.

Her reaction was even more sympathetic than Bill had expected. "Oh, I wish we could adopt him! Let's ask Padre Antonio tomorrow what he thinks about it!"

"Adopt him?" Bill was astonished.

"Why not? One more in the family wouldn't make too much difference," she urged, liking the idea more every minute.

"I'll talk to the padre," he finally promised, "but don't say anything to the girls about it yet. They'd descend on the good father in a mob and have him saying Yes before he had a chance to consider it carefully."

"All right," she agreed, and went about the job of chasing everyone to his or her room to get ready for the trip to Holiday Town and the benefit.

And after the usual confusion, scurrying around, lost articles, last minute harmonizing by the four girls, and counting of noses, the household departed for town in the crowded station wagon, with Juan wedged in happily between Billy and Pat, with little Joey on his lap. Even baby Anne went along on Nana's lap, and Mimi in her prettiest little party dress, looking like a four-year-old angel, cuddled against Mommy's shoulder sound asleep in spite of the excited chatter.

The picturesque big outdoor theatre with its rows of wooden benches climbing halfway up the geranium-grown hill, was filled to capacity for the benefit. The whole town was there—except for certain bedraggled pirates who were locked up in the coast guard's modern guardhouse at the other end of the island.

All evening the town had been waiting for the Lennon sisters to appear on the stage. And when they did, the applause could be heard almost all the way to the guardhouse. And after each number that they sang, it was louder and more prolonged.

The girls had to give several encores before the audience would let them go, and one of the heaviest applauders was the dignified, white-haired man with the young face who stood beside Frank Lane over on the far side of the big amphitheatre.

"Aren't they the greatest?" Lane demanded, as the final hand-clappers gave up trying to woo the tired singers back once more.

"Wonderful!" David Gardner said sincerely.

"Let's go backstage now. They'll be delighted to meet you. They don't know you're here."

But David Gardner shook his head. "No, I think I would rather go out to the ranch tomorrow to see them. Mr. Lennon would insist on my spending the night there, if I met him tonight. And I don't feel up to it. I'll go out with you for a quick visit tomorrow, settle with them to take the place free and clear now, and then fly back to New York at once."

Frank Lane was disappointed, but he understood how painful it must be for Gardner to revive old memories. "I suppose that will be best," he agreed regretfully. "I'll drive you out whenever you want to go."

It took the Lennon household a long time to settle down for the night, after they got back to the ranch. The girls, laden with huge bouquets, were full of happy memories of the evening, all of which had to be discussed in gay detail. There were visits back and forth between their rooms, and much running about until their elders put a stop to it and Bill Lennon sternly ordered, "Lights out!" And even then, the whispering and giggling went on for some time after their parents' door was closed.

But there was little sleep for Juan, as he watched the moon travel across the sky and finally pale and disappear in the dawnlight. He had had the most exciting day of his life with his newly found friends, and soon he would be going to a fine school and would have a chance to make something of himself, be someone his father would be proud of some day.

At last he was sleepy, but it seemed to him that he had

hardly dropped off, before Pat and Danny were knocking on his bedroom door, telling him it was time to get up for church.

Padre Antonio saw Juan's smiling face as the boy came out of church later that morning. He was walking between Kathy and Peggy, who both stopped to pose with him for the cameras of several young fans. And the padre got a little private chuckle when he saw that Janet managed to draw him away to walk with *her* while Peggy and Kathy were surrounded by autograph collectors.

It was good to see the boy so happy, especially when he was to have bad news later in the day. "At least, we will wait until after the good dinner to tell him," the good father decided privately. "It will be less of a shock, perhaps, on a full stomach!" Besides which, Padre Antonio wanted to enjoy the Lennon cooking peacefully himself!

So the big noonday dinner was a gay and happy time, and Padre Antonio enjoyed it to the last morsel of Nana's apple pie. But before he could bring himself to interrupt Juan's first game of croquet on the front lawn, and call him aside to talk to him about Bernardo, company arrived. And the interview had to be postponed for a time.

The croquet game was forgotten as the girls gathered

around excitedly to meet David Gardner, and in turn present Juan Lopez to him.

David Gardner had heard the story of their adventure a dozen times since yesterday afternoon, but he listened approvingly as Janet went over it again, and drew Juan into the telling.

"And you are their cousin?" he asked Juan. All the stories he had heard had succeeded in confusing him a bit.

"No, sir. My father is the fisherman Bernardo Lopez," Juan told him, with a smile.

But a few minutes later, as David Gardner and Frank Lane sat in the cool big library and talked with Bill Lennon and Father Anthony, the good padre brought out the letter he had received from Bernardo Lopez, and read it to them.

"Poor youngster!" David Gardner paced the floor. "I don't envy you your job telling him that Lopez not only isn't his father, but has abandoned him in the bargain!"

"Maybe in time the wound will heal, with the help of the Lennon family," Padre Antonio said, sighing.

"We'll do our best, Padre," Bill Lennon assured him.

David Gardner turned abruptly to face Bill. "Let me help financially! I'm a rich man. I can send the boy to the finest college in the country! I want to do it!"

Bill Lennon shook his head slowly. "Thanks, but we can take care of it, Mr. Gardner. It was Janet's life he saved."

"But—" David Gardner walked to the window and stared out for a minute before he turned to face them again. "You see, if my boy hadn't been taken from me, he would have been just about this boy's age now. It's for Johnny's sake I want to help this youngster."

"It would be a splendid memorial," Padre Antonio said gravely. "Think it over, Mr. Lennon, before you refuse to share this good deed."

Before Lennon could answer, there was a sound of running feet and giggling in the hallway outside, and then at least half a dozen youngsters went rioting up the stairs. "Come on, let's look through the telescope, Juan! Maybe we'll see another pirate ship!" they heard Janet's voice. And the stampede went through the upper hallway to the big front bedroom.

"My telescope! I'd almost forgotten it!" David Gardner smiled.

Bill Lennon got up quickly. "I'd better see that they don't wreck it!" He went briskly toward the door, smiling. "Never know what'll happen with that gang of mine!"

"I'll go up with you," David Gardner said suddenly.

"There may be some other things I have almost forgotten up there. I may want to ship them East with me."

The telescope was in no immediate danger. Janet was letting each of the younger ones take a turn looking out to sea through it, carefully checking to see that no sticky fingerprints were left on it.

But Juan, after one glance through the glass, had seemed more interested in the rest of the room. He was standing now in front of the handsome big desk near the hall door, studying it with an odd expression.

Janet left the telescope and came over to him. "Watcha lookin' at?" she asked. "It's just a desk with all the drawers locked. And there's no key."

Juan didn't seem to hear her. And just as David Gardner and Bill Lennon paused in the doorway, looking smilingly at the line-up at the telescope, Juan put out his hand and reached around the side of the desk, to press a hidden button. There was a sliding sound, and the deep center drawer opened.

David Gardner held back a startled exclamation and gripped Bill Lennon's arm. His face was white.

Juan took a small clown doll out of the drawer. It was old and shabby and its face was faded, but once it had had a

bright red nose to match its garments.

Janet exclaimed under her breath, "Why, it's the same one that's in the painting!" But no one noticed her. They were all looking at Juan, who was studying the doll with a puzzled expression.

"Blinkins!" Juan said, staring at the little old doll. "It's Blinkins!"

"Johnny!" David Gardner crossed the room in one big step. "No! It isn't possible!" His eyes searched Juan's face desperately as he gripped the boy's arm. Juan shrank back, frightened.

Bill Lennon hurried over, and the kids gathered around silently to stare curiously.

"My boy's first toy—how did you know what he called it?" Gardner asked Juan. "How did you know where that hidden spring was?" But Juan only stared at him.

"What seems to be wrong?" Tall Padre Antonio stood on the threshold. Juan ran to him, and the padre put his arm over the boy's shoulders.

Bill explained quickly, and Padre Antonio nodded gravely as he finished. "Perhaps it is not so strange as you think that the boy should know these things. There was a word in Bernardo Lopez' letter which might explain, though we thought little of it until now. He mentions that he found the boy 'abandoned.' It could have been in one of the coves on this very island. The boy could have been swept ashore safely after your ship was wrecked!"

And when they contacted Bernardo Lopez for the full story, that is how it turned out to have been.

And after the first shock of learning that he was not Bernardo's real son, Juan gratefully accepted his new status as John Gardner with no real regrets.

The girls were delighted for his sake and Mr. Gardner's, but when both Juan and his father begged the family to spend the rest of the summer as their guests, they were not so sure they wished to.

Dianne told her parents at a family council, "We all think it would be better for Juan—I mean, Johnny—to get acquainted with his father without our gang being around. Don't we, girls?"

And all three of the girls agreed heartily, though Kathy hesitated a little. However, once it was decided that Johnny would be going to their high school next term, she was quite happy about it.

And Janet said saucily, "Now we never will get to use the phone! But that's okay, Kath. We like him too!"

And a few days later, they were happily on their way to Uncle Max and Aunt Helen's ranch and looking forward to their usual happy, peaceful summer there. But they talked about Holiday Island for a long time afterwards, and still got a thrill out of remembering how they had taken part in solving the secret of the old ranch, which started out so spookily and ended so happily.

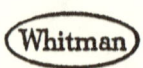

Whitman

*Famous
Classics*

Alice in Wonderland

Fifty Famous Fairy Stories

Little Men

Robinson Crusoe

Five Little Peppers and How They Grew

Treasure Island

The Wonderful Wizard of Oz

The Three Musketeers

Robin Hood

Heidi

Little Women

Black Beauty

Huckleberry Finn

Tom Sawyer

Meet wonderful friends—in the books
that are favorites—year after year

Fiction for Young People

THE RIFLEMAN

THE RESTLESS GUN

WAGON TRAIN

GENE AUTRY
The Ghost Riders

WYATT EARP

GUNSMOKE

ROY ROGERS
The Enchanted Canyon

DALE EVANS
Danger in Crooked Canyon

ROY ROGERS AND DALE EVANS
River of Peril

DRAGNET

BOBBSEY TWINS
Merry Days Indoors and Out
At the Seashore
In the Country

WALTON BOYS
Gold in the Snow
Rapids Ahead

ANNIE OAKLEY
Danger at Diablo
Double Trouble

NOAH CARR, YANKEE FIREBRAND

LEE BAIRD, SON OF DANGER

CIRCUS BOY
Under the Big Top
War on Wheels

HAVE GUN, WILL TRAVEL

MAVERICK

ASSIGNMENT IN SPACE
WITH RIP FOSTER

DONNA PARKER
At Cherrydale
Special Agent
On Her Own

TROY NESBIT'S
MYSTERY ADVENTURES
The Diamond Cave Mystery
Mystery at Rustlers' Fort

RED RYDER
Adventures at Chimney Rock

RIN TIN TIN
Rinty
Call to Danger
The Ghost Wagon Train

FURY
The Mystery at Trappers' Hole

LASSIE
Mystery at Blackberry Bog
The Secret of the Summer
Forbidden Valley

WALT DISNEY
Spin and Marty
Spin and Marty, Trouble at Triple-R

TRIXIE BELDEN
The Gatehouse Mystery
The Red Trailer Mystery
The Mystery off Glen Road
The Mysterious Visitor
Mystery in Arizona

Adventure! Mystery! Read these exciting
stories written especially for young readers